SINS OF A REBEL

PREQUEL

USA TODAY BESTSELLING AUTHOR
BROOKE O'BRIEN

SINS OF A REBEL

USA Today Bestselling author Brooke O'Brien takes you back to Carolina Beach with A Rebels Havoc in this brother's best friend, rock star prequel romance.

Kyla Cole is my best friend's sister, which makes her completely off limits.

She's sassy, sweet, and has a body made for sin.

All these years I've kept her at a distance. I'm not blind. I notice the way she looks at me, her lingering stares from across the room. If her brother had any idea about the things I've dreamed of doing with her, I'd never make it out alive.

I've heard it countless times. No one like her could ever possibly love me.

I warned her to stay away from me, but she's never been one to listen. The more I'm around her, the harder it is for me to remember all the reasons why.

We're playing a dangerous game going down this road.

I've never been one to play by the rules.

Thank you for reading **SINS OF A REBEL**! I hope you love Tysin and Kyla's story as much as I do.

You can join my Facebook group, Brooke O'Brien's Rebel Readers Group, to discuss the series and get sneak peeks on future releases. Sign up for my newsletter to find out more about my new releases. To join, visit: www.author-brookeobrien.com/followbrooke

Happy reading!

A REBELS HAVOC SERIES
READING ORDER

BRIX

a stepbrother, enemies to lovers, rock star romance

SINS OF A REBEL

a summer fling, brother's best friend, rock star romance

TYSIN

a brother's best friend, forced proximity, rock star romance

TREY

a surprise pregnancy, virgin heroine, rock star romance

MADDEN

a frenemies to lovers, journalist/rock star romance

Learn more and purchase your copy at:
www.authorbrookeobrien.com/arebelshavoc

AUTHOR'S NOTE

Dear Reader,

Thank you for grabbing your copy of Sins of a Rebel. This book is an optional prequel novella to and does end in a cliffhanger.

Like real life, Tysin and Kyla are far from perfect. They make morally gray decisions and their story deals with subjects that may be sensitive for some readers. If you're looking for a safe romance, this book is not for you.

While the rest of the A Rebels Havoc series can be read as standalones, if you prefer to read in order, it's recommended you start with Brix as the stories to inter-connect.

You can find all my books, along with recommended reading order, on my website at www.authorbrookeobrien.com.

I hope you love Tysin and Kyla as much as I do! Happy reading!

Brooke

DEDICATION

11:11

If you're searching for a sign, here's yours.
Now make a wish.

CHAPTER ONE

KYLA

"Goddamn, Kyla."

I shoot upright, dropping the fistful of cotton in my hand back into the cardboard box on the floor. The husky voice turns into a low growl, coming from somewhere in the shop. I'd recognize the deep timbre anywhere. Not for reasons one might think after his comment, but Lord knows I wish it were.

"You sure know how to greet a man, baby." He groans from behind me, this time closer than before.

My heart hammers so hard it could pound right out of my chest.

I can't remember a time in my life when I wasn't in love with Tysin Briggs. I've loved him for as long as he's been best friends with my brother, Madden.

My head slowly turns over my shoulder, and I'm met with piercing dark brown eyes. I could get lost in the creamy chocolate morsels framed by his beautiful feather-like eyelashes. Women pay a lot of money for lashes like his.

Those eyes with his sharp jaw, almost appearing as if it were crafted from a chisel, and his full lips are a total package.

Tysin wreaks havoc on my heart.

My heart skips a beat when the edge of his lip curls, showing a hint of a smile.

If I hadn't grown up around Tysin, seeing the light-hearted jokester who loved to mess with his friends, I'd wonder if he had a sense of humor at all. Since his grandmother passed away, he's grown more closed off, detached, and, to anyone who doesn't know him, seemingly uncaring.

The distant and mysterious vibe created a thick allure hanging over me like a fog whenever he was around. For years, I've wanted to chip away at the hard exterior he works so hard to keep in place with everyone around him.

I turn to face him, finding him leaning against the counter on one elbow. His eyes slowly trail down my body, smoldering like a fire into every inch and every curve. I can't be certain, but I swear I hear him release a low, shuddered breath.

"What'd you do that for?"

Raising my brow, I follow his eyes to glance down behind me, then back up to him again.

"Do what?"

"I happened to enjoy the view I was getting a moment ago. It was … nice." He grins. "Very nice."

"Nice? Just nice?"

"I'm not at liberty to say any more than that, Ky. I happen to know a lumberjack twice my size stomping around this town like Paul fuckin' Bunyan. He'd have my ass drowning in the ocean if he knew the thoughts circling my mind about his sweet little sister."

I suck in a sharp breath.

He's right. Madden made it clear to Tysin and Brix years ago that one thing was off-limits.

Me.

Except his warning was issued a long time ago. I'm an adult, fully capable of making my own decisions, and dammit, if I don't want to know what he thinks when he sees me.

"He doesn't have to know," I suggest, the words out of my mouth before I have a chance to stop them. I bite down on my lower lip to keep from saying anything more.

I peer up at Tysin from beneath my lashes, my eyes burning into his. Somehow, I don't even know how it's possible, but his stare darkens, heating my skin.

I wanted to take a step closer to Tysin, eliminate the space between us and beg him to drag me out of here. I don't know what came over me or what spell he had me under, but the look in his gaze had me yearning for him in ways that would make even the guiltiest sinner blush.

As if a snap of two fingers jerked him out of a trance, he takes a step away from me, pulling us out of the passion-fueled haze.

"Is Garrett here?" he asks, changing the subject entirely.

I force a heavy breath into my lungs and grip the edge of the counter, shaking my head feverishly.

"He should be back any minute, though. He ran to the bank before they closed."

Tysin nods, gazing out the open French doors overlooking the patio leading down to the dock near the water. The smell of the salt water lingers in the air, mixed with the familiar scent of coconut.

It's early on a Saturday morning. Despite it being summer, the locals and tourists haven't hit the beach yet, making for a quiet morning at Breaking Waves. I'm surprised to see Tysin here, especially after playing at Whiskey Barrel last night.

Tysin is the lead guitarist for A Rebels Havoc, alongside my brother, Madden, and their best friend, Brix. They've made a name for themselves around Carolina Beach and the local towns, playing shows on the weekends during summer.

"What are you doing here so early?"

"I need to talk to Garrett about a friend who's gonna help me fix my motorcycle."

He steps around me, resting his body against the wood counter spanning the wall of the store, and crosses his arms in front of him. He glances around the small cabana-style shop catering to surfers and beachgoers.

Tysin's hair is longer on top, disheveled and sticking up in all different directions. He's dressed in a dark red T-shirt and a pair of jeans. He looks relaxed and carefree.

Never mind the fact he'd fit in better in a motorcycle shop, but something about the contrast appeals to me even more.

"I guess I'll just wait here with you until he returns ..." He trails off, getting a glimpse of my swimsuit underneath my neon-purple tank top. I opted for my torn denim shorts, hanging low on my hips, showing off the tan I've been working on all summer.

It isn't that I mind having him here or that he's watching me.

If I'm being honest with myself, it's the opposite. Something about having his eyes on me makes me feel things I haven't felt with any other man.

"How am I supposed to focus with you standing there looking at me like that?"

"Like what? What am I doing?" He holds his hand to his chest, feigning innocence.

He manages to keep a straight face, but I'm no fool.

"You know what you're doing." I flash a smug smile. "You can't turn your charm on me and expect me not to see right through it. You know the effect you have on women, Sin. I've seen them around you before," I joke, noting the nickname given to him by his adoring fans.

What was once excitement turned into unease coiling tight in my stomach at the mention of him with another woman. I've always hated watching him give them attention when I wanted it on me. Just last night, before they went on stage, I saw him flirting with another girl.

I met up with my best friend, Ivy, at Whiskey Barrel. She's back in town for the summer, so to welcome her home, we hit up their show. After they wrapped, a line of Havoc Harlots waited for any of the guys to bite.

I didn't stick around long enough to watch who they took home. Although, judging by the phone call from Ivy this morning when she woke up to find Brix passed out on the couch, it's safe to say the fun didn't stop there.

Tysin's brows tightened at the change in my tone. "Doesn't mean those women have the same effect on me. It takes someone special to do that."

I would've expected his retort to be met with one of his toe-curling smirks, leaving me shedding my worries and roping me back into him. It worked, except there was no smirk to follow.

No, his face is determined, unyielding, making it clear he meant every word.

"Don't lie. You love their attention as much as they love giving it to you."

He pushes off the counter and takes me by surprise when he steps forward, eliminating the distance between us and pinning me against the hard wood. He leaves me with nowhere to go, not that I'd want to.

"What do you know about what I like?"

His nostrils flare, his lips parting.

Me? I'm stuck, frozen in place at the sight of him mere inches away from my face. All thoughts are out the window when I inhale a deep breath and am met with the captivating smell of his cologne. It's an interesting woodsy scent mixed with the smell of fresh linen.

I find myself leaning in closer, wanting more of him.

Isn't that always the case, though? I can never get enough of Tysin anytime he's around.

"You're right," I mutter, catching him off guard. "I don't know what you like or what you want."

His brow furrows.

I wish I could read his mind. My heart beats wildly, each second of silence between us ticking by at an agonizingly slow pace.

He rests his hands on the counter, not leaving an inch separating us.

I'm finding it hard to keep up with the change in his demeanor and the way he's looking at me now.

"Would it help if I told you?" he whispers.

My skin flushes, and I dart my tongue out to wet my dry lips. I nod, almost too enthusiastically, attempting to force a breath through my nose while mentally telling myself to pull my shit together.

I nod again. "Yes, I guess it would."

He smiles this time. It's not a small smile either, stretching slowly across his face. He drags his lip between his teeth before leaning close to my ear. His breath heats the side of my face, causing me to shiver.

"You, Kyla. Always you."

His voice is deep, throaty, and my eyes flutter shut.

I want to beg him to repeat those words out of fear I heard him wrong.

I don't, though. Instead, I reach my hand between us, gripping the front of his shirt, and hold him against me.

He lifts his hand, tucking a strand of hair out of my face, and brushes his thumb over the apple of my cheek.

It's the moment. The one when he kisses me.

We're alone together with no one around.

No Madden. No friends. No crazed harlots.

Just me and him.

He rubs his thumb over my lip, and I silently beg him to make the move. My tongue darts out, following the same path his finger just made, when the sound of Shinedown blares around us.

He grits his teeth and swears under his breath, pulling away. Taking a step back, he reaches into his pocket, lifting his phone to his ear.

"Yeah?" he answers in way of greeting.

"I thought I told you to get your ass here at ten?" the voice hollers. "I need that money right now. I don't have all day to wait on your sorry ass."

Tysin's jaw clenches. I recognize the voice on the other end of the line, cold and husky from years of cigarettes.

His mother.

To say their relationship is rocky would be an understatement. It's no secret Tysin despises her, and from the things I've heard over the years, the feeling is mutual.

"I told you I'd be there this afternoon. I've got shit to do."

Tysin's eyes flash over to mine, and a muscle ticks in his jaw. He searches my gaze as if looking for a sign I may have heard her. I turn away, giving him privacy to finish his conversation.

I bend down to grab the T-shirt I tossed in the box earlier and resume folding them.

"Listen here, you little piece of shit." I hear again, and my eyes go wide.

My heart seizes in my chest at the thought of him being on the receiving end of her wrath.

"Goodbye," he barks.

The silence that follows is deafening. I toss the shirt on the counter and turn back toward him.

He looks different, like the young boy I remember him being the first time we met. I'm not sure if he's angry, hurt, or embarrassed. Maybe a little of all three.

"Tysin," I say, breaking through the stillness around us.

"Please don't," he grits out.

I press my lips together, hating how quickly things shifted from hot to cold.

"I need to take off." He runs his hand through his hair, turning toward the door. "When Garret gets back, can you tell him I dropped by and to give me a call?"

"You bet."

He stops when he reaches the door, turning back to look at me. Our eyes stay locked for a moment, long enough to notice the spark of an indefinable emotion before he nods, disappearing out the door.

For the next hour, I replay every second of our time together.

You, Kyla. Always you.

CHAPTER TWO

TYSIN

I know the risk of what I'm about to do, but I don't give a shit anymore.

I've held myself back from Kyla out of fear of ruining my friendship with Madden. When I walked into Breaking Waves and saw her standing there—her smooth skin and soft smile, her eyes glittering with happiness merely at the sight of me—I couldn't stop myself.

I haven't been able to stop thinking about anything else since.

Madden doesn't have to know.

Kyla's different than all the women who hang around after our shows. Shit, I knew that years ago. She's never cared about what anyone else thought of her. She marches to the beat of her own drum, which has always drawn me to her.

She's loyal as hell to the people in her life. If you were someone close to her, you knew it too. She didn't give up or turn her back on the people she loved.

She's the real deal. The ride or die type.

I glance up when she steps out the door. Her long lavender hair is down, and she's wearing a pair of bright red retro-styled sunglasses. She has a style uniquely Kyla. Her colorful tattoos span the length of her arms like an edgy pin-up model, and goddamn does she always have my eyes burning on her. I want to soak up every inch of her body and those curves she barely keeps covered.

She doesn't notice me at first. Her eyes are trained on her phone when she reaches for her keys out of her pocket, looking up to hit the unlock when her gaze finally meets mine.

Her steps falter, coming to a complete stop.

I wish I could see the look in her eyes or know what she was thinking when she saw me leaning against the tailgate of my pickup parked next to her.

If the slow breathtaking grin across her face is any indication, though, I'd say it's a good sign she's happy to see me.

"Back to see Garrett?"

I shake my head. "Not this time."

"Is that right?" She snickers.

The parking lot is full of people, and we are interrupted when a car pulls in, passing between us. When the coast is clear, she jogs over and stops a few feet from me.

"What brought you here this time?"

She rakes her teeth over her lip, attempting to cover the smile playing at the edge of her mouth. No matter how much she tries to fight it, she gives in.

I've always loved seeing how her body reacts whenever she's around me.

I'm not blind. I've noticed how her eyes linger on me, especially when she knows Madden isn't paying attention. He may not have noticed, but I know for a fact Brix has.

He's given me shit about it for months.

"You thinkin' about picking up surfing?"

"Nah." I chuckle. "You'd never catch me on one of those things. I have a better idea. You up for it?" I ask, nodding toward my pickup.

She pulls her sunglasses off, and this time, she doesn't hide her excitement.

"Where are we going?"

I haven't thought this through until she climbs into the front seat next to me.

I take all the same familiar roads leading to my house near the water. It's probably not a good idea, considering the guys always drop by my place.

It's where we leave our equipment and practice. I moved in with my grandmother when I was fifteen, needing to get away from my mom. When my grandmother passed away a year later, she left me her house and an inheritance to help care for me until I turned eighteen.

It made the most sense for us to practice at my place since I had the space and no one around to be bothered by our loud music.

"I guess I hadn't thought that far ahead."

"We could always go down to the boardwalk, maybe find somewhere on the beach away from the crowd to hang out."

"You're already trying to get me alone?" I jest.

"Yes." She grins.

I'm not sure what I expected her to say or how she'd act now that the two of us are alone again. When she reaches for the hem of her tank top and pulls it over her head, I'm grateful I have half a mind to check I'm still driving on the road before my gaze darts back to her.

She reaches over, turning the volume up on the radio before resting her body against the door. She leans her head and arm out the window, soaking in the sunshine and letting the warm breeze wash over her.

Something about her carefree side shined like a beacon of light on all the dark corners of my world.

I couldn't let myself think about how wrong I was for her, but dammit if I didn't wish it were different.

I had the chance to be with Kyla, to have her alone and all to myself. I was going to take it and hold on to it with every ounce of strength in me.

When we pull down by the beach, rows of cars are parked along the pier. Surfboards line the strip. People relax on their beach towels with children laughing in the background as the waves crash into them, washing up onto the shoreline.

"This isn't what I had in mind when you said alone." I chuckle, glancing out the window as teenagers climb out of a packed car with their beach bags and towels in hand, taking off toward the water.

"Me either." She giggles, tilting her head back against the headrest. "We could always walk farther down toward the pier. It's a little less crowded that way."

"Let's do it," I say.

I'm thankful I decided to swap out my jeans for a pair of shorts and a tank top. Otherwise, I would've stuck out like a sore thumb.

I pull my hat down on my head and slip on my sunglasses, hoping not to draw any unwanted attention.

We slip off our shoes, letting our feet sink into the warm sand. The sun starts to disappear behind the clouds, leaving the sky overcast. Word on the radio this morning talked about a storm rolling in.

The farther we get away from the water, the more distant the sound of laughter is, replaced with the water lapping against the coastline. We stand next to each other, lost in thought as we stare off into the distance at the colliding waves.

The approaching storm is turning the sky a mixture of dark blue and purple.

"Looks like the storm will be here before too long. I should've picked a better day, huh?"

She shrugs, lifting her hand to her eyes to shield her from the sun peeking through the clouds. "I think it's perfect."

She reaches for the button on her shorts, sashaying her hips until they drop around her ankles. My eyes drink in the sight of her smooth sun-kissed skin covering her hips up to the ink marking her arms. She's wearing an aqua-blue swimsuit with white ruffles over the edge of her top.

She breaks out into nervous laughter before taking off toward the water.

I'm left standing there, mesmerized by the sound. The waves smack into her legs, sending her falling over before she dives in.

"You coming?" she hollers, running her hand through her wet hair before wiping her face.

I pull my shirt over my head and toss it to the ground. I lift my eyes, and our gaze connects. She fights off a grin as I push my pants down my legs, leaving me in my black boxer briefs.

She watches intently, a shade of pink highlighting her cheeks.

The cool water is a much-needed reprieve from the scorching temperatures we've been dealing with lately. When I reach the water, I dive in, heading straight toward Kyla.

She yelps when my hands circle her waist, pulling her into my arms. She slips her arms around my neck, her legs following suit around my hips.

I snap my mouth shut when she grinds her pussy against my dick.

"Jesus Christ, Kyla," I mumble. My fingers grip her ass, desperate to hold her still.

She smirks, loving the way she's driving me crazy. If she were anyone else, I'd be untying those bottoms and fucking her right here on the beach, not caring who's around to watch.

"Tell me something about you, Tysin."

She locks her fingers around my neck and tilts her head back, letting her hair dip into the water before meeting my eyes once more.

"Like what?" I croak.

"I feel like I know the version of Tysin the rest of the world gets to see. Tell me something no one knows about you."

She's digging in deeper, wanting to get a glimpse inside the person I am under the surface. I don't know how I feel about it.

I shrug. "Not much to tell, honestly."

She narrows her eyes, shaking her head. "I don't believe you. We all have parts of ourselves we don't share with others, at least not with strangers. Sometimes you seem like a stranger to me. I want to know the real Tysin."

I chuckle, sifting through my mind to find something to share with her.

"Am I making you nervous?" she asks.

"Not for reasons you might think." I drop my gaze between us.

She pulls herself closer to me, her chest pressing against mine.

"You make me nervous too," she admits.

Her lips are red from the water's cooler temperatures, with water droplets over her face and chest.

"I can sing."

Her eyes widen in awe. "Wait, really?"

I nod. "It's not something I like to do publicly, but I can."

"How come you don't sing with the guys?"

"Brix likes to be the center of attention. It's not my thing. Don't get me wrong, I enjoy singing and think I'm pretty good at it, but I don't mind Brix being the only one who fills that role."

She shakes her head in amazement. "I never would've guessed. Do the guys know?"

I nod. "We've talked about the two of us singing before or even me filling in on backup vocals. I don't mind things staying the way they are, though. We have a good thing goin', so why mess it up?"

I run my hands over her hips, my fingers gripping into her thighs, using her body to distract me from the conversation.

"Will you sing for me?" she asks. She looks up at me with her soft smile, making it difficult to say no.

"I haven't practiced for a while, so I'm a bit rusty. One day I will, though."

She sighs. "You promise?"

I lean in close to her. Her breasts press against my chest, and I'm still distracted by her pussy rubbing against my dick. My warm breath feathers over her ear, and she tilts her head to the side, giving me better access.

Brushing my lips against her skin causes her body to shudder beneath me. I trail kisses toward her neck, then nip at her earlobe.

"I promise."

CHAPTER THREE

TYSIN

"You comin'?" Kyla sings, spinning around toward me, wearing a wide smile.

Her purple hair sticks to the side of her face as she twirls around, her arms out wide as the rain beats down around us.

The sight of her infectious smile and the sound of her laugh are like a balm to my battered soul. Drops of rain fall from her lashes, and her top clings to her in ways I craved to be wrapped around her body.

"Hurry up," she urges, waving her hand toward me. She bounces on the pad of her feet, skipping ahead toward my truck.

She shakes her head when she turns back, finding me stalking toward her.

"I don't run," I quip.

She rolls her eyes and reaches her hand out for me, tugging me toward her. I push her against the door, my arms trapping her in and leaving her with nowhere to run.

"Not even for me?" she whispers, staring up at me. Her chest heaves, and I lean in, meeting her gaze, then let my eyes trail down to her lips.

She sucks in a sharp breath. I want to kiss her so badly, but I know once I do, there will be no going back.

I won't be able to stop, not that I want to either.

"Tysin." Her low voice tugs at me as if coaxing me to give in.

"Kyla, I don't think …" I can't even say the words because I know it's a lie.

Her eyes search mine, looking for the answer, and I shake my head.

She reaches out, gripping the front of my shirt as rain continues to fall around us.

"Say it. Whatever you're thinking, just say it."

I shake my head. "No."

With a sigh, she drops her arms to her side, clearly misreading the conflict tormenting my thoughts. She thinks I'm pushing her away, rejecting her, but I'm not.

I'm fighting a war within myself because I want her so badly.

I'm damn near ready to order her into my pickup and take her right here, right now.

"It's okay," she says. "Can you take me back to my car?"

She attempts to move past me, but my arms are still around her, and I'm not willing to let her go. Not when she has it all wrong.

Reaching for her hips, I press her back against the door. I tilt her chin up toward me, and without allowing myself to second-guess it again, I crash my lips down on hers.

She moans when I reach up, wrapping my hand around her throat. She opens up to me, her tongue brushing along mine. I rock my hips against her, and her body shudders.

"God, you're killing me, Kyla," I mutter, squeezing my eyes shut.

I tilt my forehead against hers and stare into her green eyes. The color is vibrant like emeralds. I tuck a strand of hair away from her face, and she relaxes into my touch.

"I shouldn't want you as badly as I do," I murmur.

She sucks in a sharp breath.

"I don't give a shit what Madden thinks," she fires off.

The certainty and grit behind her words are as if she'd go to battle if he dares to get in the way. Kyla has always been one to fire back at Madden, and I know without a doubt she'd tell him off if he threatened to come between us.

That's not the point, though. I know she believes he's the reason I'm holding back.

Kyla deserves the world. She's the type of girl you only find once in your lifetime. When you find her, you better hold her tight.

I'm the guy your brothers warn you to stay away from. I'm selfish and fucked up. I'm not capable of loving a woman the way she deserves to be loved.

I'd destroy her and her heart, shattering her in a million pieces.

There's no going back once we cross this line, but fuck me, I can't help myself.

I'm a selfish bastard, and even if it's only for one night, I want to taste her. To have her in my arms.

"Get in the truck, Kyla."

She sighs and nods, moving to circle around the front to the passenger side. I wrap my arm around her waist, like a rubber band snapping her back to me.

"Nuh-uh," I whisper into her again.

She rocks her ass against my dick.

"You like feeling how fuckin' hard I am because of you?"

She nods and arches her back, grinding against me again. I grit my teeth to steel off the string of curse words from flowing out of my mouth.

"Don't tease me, Kyla."

Her body trembles. "Or what?"

I grin, knowing it's exactly what she wants.

She's baiting me, wanting to find out what will happen if she continues. If I give in, she'll only torture me more.

"I said get in the truck," I command, reaching for the door handle.

She climbs into the driver's side, her ass swaying in the air when she moves to the center, giving me room to follow.

Clenching my teeth, I don't bother to adjust myself, trying to avoid drawing attention to the steel rod in my pants.

The slow smile that stretches across her face, though, confirms she sees it.

I reach down to adjust the seat, giving her room between me and the steering wheel, and she takes it, climbing over me to straddle my lap.

There's no hope for me getting out of this easily now. I've unleashed the monster, and I'll have to atone for my sins.

Goose bumps break across her skin. She leans up on her knees, pulling her shirt over her head before dropping it on the floor.

"I'm wet," she whispers.

I fight off the urge to slip my fingers inside her bikini bottoms to find out how wet she truly is.

My hand slides over her cheek, pulling her back to me, and I steal another kiss. I rake my other fingers over her thigh, and she swivels her hips, rubbing her heat over my dick.

I inhale a sharp breath when I pull back. Blush highlights the apples of her cheeks.

Checking out our surroundings, I make sure no one can see. What was once a packed parking lot full of beachgoers has been left empty. The windows fog from our heavy panting.

My fingers brush along the edge of her bikini top, pulling the material down to free her breast. The cool air against her damp skin causes her nipples to harden. I suck my finger into my mouth and flick it over her puckered flesh.

My nostrils flare at the sight, picturing her doing the same thing with her tongue around the tip of my dick.

"Kyla," I warn. She opens her mouth, lifting my finger to her lips, and drags her tongue over the length before moving it back to her nipple. She tilts her head back and sighs again.

"Sin."

My name rolls out slow and breathy, full of need.

I give in. Consequences be damned.

I lean forward, lapping my tongue over her nipple, and suck her into my mouth. Her breath stutters, digging her fingers into my hair and tugging on the strands.

I struggle to keep it together, running my hands over her thighs.

When I rub my finger over her clit through the material, she releases a heavy moan mixed with the word, "Please."

I slowly trace the edge of her bottoms, and she leans back, attempting to give me more room. I pull her swimsuit to the side, giving me better access.

When I drag my finger over her clit and down to her entrance, I watch as it disappears into her tight heat. The sight of her wetness glistening on my finger, mixed with her groans, makes it impossible to contain the urge to lay her out across the bench seat and take her now.

I need to help her finish, so I can get the fuck out of here.

I rub my thumb over her clit as I curl my finger inside her to rub that sweet spot.

Her mouth falls open, her eyes rolling closed when she does, and her breath comes out in uneven pants.

She digs her nails into my forearm, grinding her pussy against the palm of my hand.

"That's it, baby," I mutter. "Take what you need from me."

"Oh fuck," she groans. "I think I'm gonna come."

I keep the same momentum, flicking my tongue over her nipple again. The combination of the three is her undoing.

She tosses her head back, her body quivering as the force of her release wracks through her. She collapses against my chest, her arms wrapping around my neck to hold me against her.

"That was … incredible." She snickers, pulling back to kiss me. "You're gonna have me addicted."

The thought crosses my mind, wondering if this is the first time she's finished with a man. I stop myself before I let my thoughts go any further. Picturing her with someone else tears me apart inside.

"I feel like this whole day has been a dream. Like any moment now, I'm going to wake up, and it'll all be taken away from me."

My chest pangs at her choice of words.

"I don't want to hurt you, Kyla."

"I know, that's not what I meant. I think I've been waiting, hoping for the day when you'd see me as more than Madden's little sister. Now that I've had this, and I know what it's like to be in your arms, I don't want to go back to what life was like before."

"I don't want to go back either," I say, honestly.

She grins, slipping her hand around the base of my neck, and kisses me. My fingers dig into her soft skin, holding her close.

I didn't want to let her go. The voices in my head were like an angel and devil on each shoulder. One was telling me I could get past my fears and prove to Madden I'm worthy of being the man Kyla deserves.

On the other hand, the devil replays the same things I've heard all my life.

No one will ever love you.

You're a piece of shit. Who could ever want you?

It's your fault your dad isn't in your life.

I'll never regret being with Kyla, even though I know I can't give her anything more than this.

When she parted her lips to kiss me again, it sent shock waves through my entire body. I give in and let myself succumb to the moment with her. If this is all I'll have with her, I want to hold on to it with both fists.

I'll never be the man Kyla deserves, but deep down, I want to be.

CHAPTER FOUR

TYSIN

"Let's call it a day," Brix mutters, shaking his head.

He's checked his phone for the fourth time since he's been here. We've butt heads countless times over the past couple of weeks since Ivy returned to town.

Ivy is Kyla's best friend and just so happens to be Brix's new stepsister.

I've been giving him shit over it since the news got out. It's no secret he wants to fuck her, but now he's stuck living in the same house with her for the summer.

He couldn't take the fact she rejected him just before they found out their parents eloped. It got under his skin so bad that he tried making a bet with me that he could sleep with her, only to send her back to school at the end of the summer heartbroken.

We both know he's full of shit.

He was an asshole to her throughout high school. He likes to play it off like he's not in knots over her, but anyone who knows him can see through his bullshit.

"Whatever, man. Get your sorry ass out of here," I grunt, lifting the strap of my guitar over my head and setting it on the stand.

His eyes narrow, shooting me a penetrating glance. He shoulders past the microphone, stepping down from our makeshift stage in the basement of my house, and makes a beeline for the stairs.

I don't realize he's taking off until he growls out, "See ya," and throws a wave over his shoulder.

"What the hell has gotten into him?" Madden croaks.

"Poison Ivy," I joke.

Madden smirks, twisting the drumsticks between his fingers, recalling the nickname Brix gave her back in high school.

"I'm gonna head home and hit the shower. Wanna meet up at Whiskey Barrel in an hour and grab a beer?" Madden asks.

Sweat drips from his brow. He uses the sleeve of his T-shirt to dab it away before stepping around his drum set.

How do I tell him no without raising any red flags?

We both know there's not shit to do around here on a Sunday night.

I've been itching to get my hands on Kyla again since our date. I've tried to keep my distance from her. As much as I've battled with myself about being with her, I haven't been able to stop thinking about getting her alone again.

"I've got some shit to do for my mom here in a little bit," I lie.

We both know how sensitive the topic of my mother is, and Madden usually treads lightly when talking about her. He doesn't normally ask too many questions.

He shakes his head, and warning bells immediately go off in my mind.

"What's that look for?"

"Your mom, man. She doesn't deserve you helping her with shit."

I shrug because he's right.

I'm all she has, though. Try as I might, I can't do to her like she's done to me.

I guess there's some part inside me that hopes one day she'll love me like a mother is supposed to.

"You're right. It's just, I know it's what Gram would want me to do if she were still here."

"One of these days, you need to start living for yourself," Madden retorts.

If only he knew how deeply those words resonated.

"You're a good man, Tysin." He claps me on the shoulder. "I'll be around if you change your mind after you go over there. Lord knows you may need that beer."

I chuckle and nod. I didn't want to say anything more. I'm not a good liar, and I have a one-track mind. All I can think about is where I could meet Kyla away from any curious eyes.

It's not easy to do in this small town.

An hour later, I'm leaning against the side of my '71 Cutlass Supreme with my arms crossed over my chest when

I spot Kyla turn the corner on her light-blue bicycle. Her curly hair whips in the wind behind her with a matching bandana tied around her head, holding the strands away from her face.

It's hard to pretend I don't want to devour her.

It feels like forever since I've had her alone. I've seen her a few times down at Whiskey Barrel when she was visiting Ivy, coming out to watch us play. We've exchanged a few texts here and there, but I didn't know where to go from here.

It's uncharted territory for me. Not to mention, it's hard as hell hiding how badly I want her with her brother only a few feet away.

I couldn't try to avoid her, but even more than that, I didn't want to anymore.

She pulls up next to me and hits the brakes, straddling her bike. She slides her cat-eye sunglasses down her nose and wags her brows at me.

"Hi." She smiles, stepping off her bike and flipping down the kickstand.

She slips her sunglasses off, hanging them from the collar of her tank. She's dressed in black denim shorts and a white top, showing off her tattoos.

She scans our surroundings, almost as if she's expecting her brother to pop out of nowhere.

"It's just me."

She nods. "I mean, I figured you wouldn't text me to meet you if he was."

I shake my head, and she smiles. Now that the coast is clear, she steps around her bike and wraps her arms around my waist.

When she pulls back, I drop my hand and lace my fingers with hers. She stares at our joined hands before peering up at me with a relaxed smile.

Sooner or later, I'd have to put a stop to this for good. For now, I wanted to ignore the demons in the back of my mind shouting at me to leave her alone.

Kyla was everything good in this world. She didn't need my darkness ruining hers.

"Come with me," I urge, tugging on her hand.

She stops me to bend down to lock her bike on one of the racks lining the boardwalk. I shove my hands into my black denim jeans, glancing down at my A Rebels Havoc shirt and my red Vans.

When I reach for her hand again, she presses her lips together to fight off her smile.

"What?" I ask.

"You do realize someone could spot us and our cover would be blown."

I shrug. She's right. In fact, it's likely someone would notice me and recognize her as Madden's sister. In a matter of minutes, rumors could begin swirling around Carolina Beach.

"I have somewhere I want to take you away from everyone."

She wags her brows suggestively. "Oh yeah?"

"Don't tempt me, Kyla."

She tosses her head back and giggles. I'm mesmerized by the sound. I grunt, pulling her close to me.

"You're not helping."

She drags her teeth over her lower lip, trying to temper her smile.

Goddamn, what is she doing to me?

The sun has started to set. The skyline along the water is a mixture of purple, pinks, and orange. There's a small ice cream stand near the water. Kyla pulls me to a stop, pointing at the ice cream cone pictured on the sign.

She settles on a chocolate and vanilla mixture, one scoop of each. I smile at the sight of her eyes lighting up when the gentleman hands her the cone, ice cream dripping down the side from the heat of the North Carolina sun.

She drags her tongue along the side, quickly catching every drop. I'm lost in thought at the sight of her.

"You want some?" she asks, holding it out to me.

I stare at the remnants left over on her lips before she quickly darts her tongue out, swiping the sweetness away.

The visual of her licking and sucking, using her tongue the way she is now, makes it harder and harder to focus.

I grumble, shaking my head before sliding my fingers down her forearm and reaching for her hand.

"You good?" She cackles, and my stare bores into her.

She knows the game she's playing by tempting me. My fingers itch to grip her by the chin and kiss the look right off her face.

We make our way down the beach. I do my best to avoid watching her finish her treat, but she makes it difficult. The summer heat isn't doing her any favors, melting it faster than she can eat.

I point my finger at the blanket I set up for us earlier along the tall grass, giving us space from the rest of the beach. Most of the crowd has dispersed, folding up their lawn chairs and towels and finding their way to the boardwalk.

The sun starts to set, and the lights from the Ferris wheel and food trucks illuminate in the distance.

"You planned this?" Her mouth falls open.

She squeezes my hand and takes a step toward me. Her chest against my front, tilting her head back to smile.

"How'd I get so lucky with you?" she whispers.

I shrug, flashing her a wink. "I'm asking myself the same thing."

I grip her chin in my fingers and crash my lips on hers. They're sticky from her treat, and when I pull back, I swipe my tongue over mine.

She pulls me down onto the blanket, giving us privacy from anyone walking by. She sits between my legs, resting her head on my shoulder, and we stare out at the water.

We sit in silence, listening to the waves lapping at the shoreline and people laughing in the distance.

"Did Madden tell you we finished recording our demo?"

She shakes her head. "That's amazing. One day, you guys are gonna take off and hit it big. I just know it!"

I raise my brows. "You think so?"

She nods enthusiastically. "I do. I've never doubted it either."

"That's my dream."

It's everything I've always wanted. To get the fuck out of this town, away from my mom, and never look back.

I used to lie awake at night and think about the day it would happen. I've busted my ass. We all have, fighting to make it a reality.

"What about you?" I ask.

"What about me?" Her face softens.

"What's your dream?"

She releases a slow breath and shrugs. You can practically see the barrage of thoughts and questions swirling through her mind. She glances back out onto the water, seeming to consider her answer.

"Finish school. Find a job. Who knows? I mean, one day I'd love to settle down and have a family, but I'm not thinking that far ahead."

She drops her eyes to her hands, moving her sunglasses still hanging from her collar to toss them onto the blanket next to us.

I wonder if she's thinking about how different our paths are.

Gritting my teeth, I shake my head, forcing it from my mind.

It didn't matter anyway. Sooner or later, this would all come to an end. All I would have to hold on to are these memories with her.

CHAPTER FIVE

KYLA

"Spill the beans, sister." I snicker.

It's been a few days since I last met up with Ivy. Even still, I'm behind on what's going on with her and in her life. The last time we spoke, she told me about the date she went on with Brix.

Ivy's eyes dart over to me, and she narrows them playfully.

"What do you want to know?" she quips.

"It seems like things progressed so quickly. You went from hating each other to what? Living in the same house to damn near ready to rip each other's clothes off. How'd it even happen?"

She wrinkles her nose, fighting off a grin.

I keep one foot planted on my board, using the other to pick up speed, weaving from side to side. The wheels of my longboard click rhythmically from the cracks on the sidewalk.

Ivy's riding along next to me, the warm breeze causing her dark hair to blow behind her.

"I'm learning there's a lot more hidden under the asshole façade he tries to play off in front of everyone else. He can be surprisingly sweet sometimes."

My eyebrows dart up. "Who would've thought?"

She chuckles. "I know, right? Who would've thought I'd ever give that prick a chance?"

"Not me." I giggle.

"What about you? You and Tysin seemed awfully cozy the other day at their band practice. What's going on between you two?"

I sigh. It's been on my mind a lot lately.

I can't help but notice how hot and cold things are with Tysin. Whenever we are alone, things are perfect. Amazing. I wouldn't change a thing about our time together.

Only the days after are different.

He's growing distant, and I'm finding myself wanting to see him more, hoping he'll message me to sneak away to meet up with him again.

We'll go days between seeing each other, sometimes without even talking. It's starting to feel like a roller coaster, and I'm ready to get off.

I knew it wouldn't be easy, especially when he's insisting on keeping things between us quiet. I don't care what my brother thinks about our relationship.

I want to be with Tysin, and sooner or later, he would have to find out.

I kept telling myself maybe if he knew, it would put a stop to the silence. Maybe Tysin would start to warm up to the idea of us being more than we are now.

I didn't want to be kept a secret forever, and it hurt that he wanted us to be.

A secret.

"I guess it depends on the day you ask me."

Ivy is a few steps ahead, but when she hears my tone, she taps her foot on the ground to slow her pace.

"Did something happen?"

I chuckle. "That's the thing. Nothing's happening. I haven't seen him in six days. We've hardly spoken to each other. I'm trying not to let it get to me, but it's eating me up inside."

"Have you tried talking to him about it?"

"No." I shrug. "I guess I'm trying not to let it get to me. Maybe if I don't acknowledge it, it'll be easier to pretend it's all in my head."

The sidewalk is thick with pedestrians walking toward the boardwalk. I slow down and step on the end of my board, reaching to carry it with me.

Ivy signals over to the snow cone stand. I nod, following her to wait our turn in line.

I wish I wouldn't have brought this up. As soon as I voiced my feelings out loud, it's as if all my fears were turned into reality.

"Hey, Kyla," a voice shouts from the distance.

I recognize his voice, sending my eyes darting over my shoulder in search of him. He whistles to catch my attention, and I spot Tysin jogging across the street toward us.

There's a music shop across the way. Madden has mentioned stopping by there a few times. I'm guessing he's down here picking something up when he saw us standing here.

"Hey." He releases a heavy breath and nods toward Ivy. "Hey, Ivy."

"Tysin." Ivy smirks. "Speak of the rebel."

His gaze bounces from her over to me, picking up on the hint we were talking about him.

His eyes travel down my body to the white crop top I'm wearing with my denim shorts. They're a size too big, sitting low on my hips, the edges frayed before he stops on my lavender checkered Vans.

He, on the other hand, is making it hard to focus. His hair is grown out longer than normal, but I like it. My fingers itch to run through the strands, tugging on the ends when he pulls me in for a kiss.

His shirt is off, slung over his shoulder, and his black jeans show a hint of the happy trail disappearing beneath his waistband.

"I'm down here with your brother." He motions toward the shop.

I nod. "I guess you gotta go then?"

I wonder if he can hear it in my voice, even though I'm fighting and failing at not letting my emotions show. His gaze flicks over to Ivy as if checking to see if she's listening, and my stomach sinks.

Why do we have to hide what's going on between us?

He takes a step toward me, reaching for my hand and lacing our fingers together. His brows deepen, staring down at where he rubs his thumb over my skin.

I want to ask what's bothering him, and he shakes his head. It's as if he can sense the question lingering in the air, but he's asking me not to say it out loud.

"Tysin." I hear shouted in the distance. The voice is familiar, and we both look to find Madden stalking toward us.

Tysin sighs and steps back, releasing my hand.

Ivy mutters under her breath, "She doesn't deserve to be kept a secret."

His brow furrows, looking back over at me.

"What are ya doin'?" Madden barks, clapping Tysin on the shoulder as he looks between the three of us.

"Where's Brix?" Ivy asks, changing the subject. "I didn't think the three of you went anywhere without each other."

"He had some business with his mom to tend to before practice, I guess," Madden says. "We're meeting him back at Tysin's in a few."

Madden doesn't notice the change in topic, and I'm thankful for the distraction. I don't doubt Ivy knows the answer to her own question, but it deflects his attention away from Tysin and me.

My mind soaks in his comment about them heading back to Tysin's place, wondering what else he's been doing since we were last together. Why hasn't he reached out to me or stopped by Breaking Waves? Has he thought about our time together or wanted to see me?

Ivy steps up to the counter and places her order, asking me if I want anything. I shake my head but then ask for a water.

I'm fighting against every urge to look at Tysin. I wonder if he feels the magnetic pull, holding me to him too. It's as if every second that ticks by and we're near each other, my body feels his presence, luring me to him.

"You ready to go?" Madden asks, elbowing Tysin before glancing at me.

For a second, I wonder if he picked up on it too, if he sensed the tension building between us. I give in and flash my eyes over to Tysin, finding him staring back at me.

My tongue darts out of my mouth, wetting my dry lips.

Where the hell is my water?

Tysin's throat bobs at the sight of my tongue. He clenches his jaw and turns toward Madden, nodding his head.

"Let's go," he replies flatly, his voice firm.

If I didn't know him better, I'd think he was angry. He's not, though, and something about knowing I have this effect on him with my brother mere inches away sends relief rushing through me.

It doesn't answer the question as to why he's been so distant lately, but the voice in the back of my mind tells me maybe there's more to it.

"See ya," they both say in unison. Tysin lifts his hand in a short wave.

Ivy turns back toward me, snow cone in hand, and hands me my bottled water. I quickly uncap the top and take a long drink as she scoops a large bite of her flavored ice into her mouth.

"Why don't you just tell Madden what's going on? Rip off the Band-Aid, so to speak." Ivy asks.

"I'm not trying to pressure things or rush it, ya know? At the same time, it's hard not to when this is what I've wanted for so long."

Ivy nods. "You don't think he's sleeping with anyone else, do you?"

The question settles like a ball of cotton lodged in my throat. I've tried not to think about it, but it's crossed my mind over the past few days.

I've thought about showing up at his place to surprise him, but I've also feared what I may walk into if I do.

"I don't know, honestly. I don't think so."

"Have you had sex yet?" Ivy asks as we step off the curb away from the line of people.

I screw the cap back on, focusing my eyes on Madden and Tysin as they cross the street on their way to Tysin's Cutlass.

When he circles the car and opens the door, he glances back over at us, and a slow smile spreads across his face when he finds me staring at him.

"Don't bother answering my question. The sexual tension between you two is so thick, it makes my pussy flutter. *Jesus!*"

I bark out a laugh, sending me into a coughing fit.

She takes another bite and shrugs, a smug smile displayed proudly on her face.

"Listen, I don't know why you two torture yourselves, but clearly, you're into each other. So what if Madden has a problem with it? He'll get over it eventually. He's your brother, for fuck's sake."

"That's how I feel, but Tysin wants things on the down low, and I don't know why. I'm almost afraid to ask him what's holding him back."

"You can't keep pushing it off, though, either. You'll drive yourself crazy."

I nod. I don't even think I'd be so bothered by keeping our relationship private for a while if it meant we kept in touch on the days when I couldn't see him.

It's the silence between that's getting to me. As the days tick by, the more doubt and dread seep into my mind, and it's a slow, torturous game.

I don't know how much longer I can take it.

"Well, it will have to come out eventually," Ivy says. "You know what they say. What happens in the dark always comes to light."

CHAPTER SIX

KYLA

The next day, it's after seven when I wrap up my shift at Breaking Waves. Garrett is closing the shop, so I'm alone when I step out the door and find Tysin leaning against the tailgate of his pickup.

My heart rate spikes at the sight of him dressed in a pair of black Dickies and a white shirt with his backward baseball cap on.

His smile spreads across his face, highlighting the dimple on his cheek.

"I wasn't expecting to see you here."

"I thought I'd try to catch you before you went home. Got plans tonight?"

It's a Sunday night, and there's not much to do but go home and hang out. I'm due back at Breaking Waves at ten tomorrow.

"Not a thing." I grin. "I guess I'm all yours."

His brows shoot up, and he reaches his hand out for mine, pulling me into his arms. He circles them around my waist. He stands almost a foot taller than me, leaning down to press a kiss against my mouth.

It's soft at first, and I melt into him, my fingers gripping the front of his shirt as if it'll save me when my legs give out beneath me.

He releases a heavy sigh when he leans back, moving to fold his hands against my cheek, deepening the kiss. This time when he kisses me, it's commanding and all-consuming, nearly stealing the breath right out of me.

I moan when he pulls back, not wanting him to stop.

"Let's go back to my place where we can have a little privacy." He smirks, his voice low and throaty.

I nod, and he laces our fingers and leads me around to his side of the truck. I quickly climb in and take the spot next to him.

He turns the ignition and rests his hand on my thigh as we pull out of the parking lot.

We make small talk the whole drive back to his house. He asks about my work shift, and I tell him about the storm that hit earlier this morning, making for a quiet day at the shop. We chat about their show the night before and the after-party he hit up with the guys.

My stomach sinks, wondering who he may have been with, before forcing the thought out of my mind.

I hate how jealous I feel when I know the lifestyle that comes along with dating a rock star.

He turns into the driveway of his little white house on the edge of Carolina Beach. His grandma owned it before she passed away, leaving it to him.

I don't know much about his home life, only the bits and pieces I've heard from Madden over the years. All I know is it was bad enough that he petitioned the court to be emancipated after she died.

He's lived here on his own ever since.

His grandma left him a good chunk of money to help take care of him. I don't know for certain, but I suspect it's why his mom treats him the way she does. She's bitter that her mother cared more about her grandson, leaving everything she had to him.

At least that's the story Madden shared with our parents one day when they asked why on earth Tysin lived in the house by himself.

He puts it in park and cuts the engine, bathing us in darkness.

There's a streetlight behind us, giving a hint of light, enough for me to see him staring at me.

"I haven't been able to stop thinking about you since the last time we were together," he whispers.

My heart seizes, and I press my lips together, knowing full well the size of my smile would give away how happy it made me to hear.

"Me either," I whisper.

He brushes his finger over the skin of my inner thigh, and my body relaxes, my legs falling open a little more.

"I promise I didn't invite you over here for any reason other than to hang out, but I'm finding it hard to resist you now that I've given in and had a taste."

I tilt my head up, resting my chin on his shoulder. I wish he'd keep going and tell me what else he's been thinking about. "You won't see me try to stop you either."

His eyes burn into my lips before he leans in and kisses me again.

"Let's go inside. I thought maybe we could watch a movie."

"Sounds good to me." I grin.

I've been to Tysin's house before, but we've always stuck to hanging out in the basement where their equipment is set up for band practice.

Being in his house, in his space, made me feel closer to him.

The walls are covered with wallpaper, a mixture of mulberries and peonies with green vines. There's a dark brown couch facing a big-screen TV with a matching recliner next to it. It's cozy and a bit outdated, not at all what you'd expect to find in Tysin's home. If I had to guess, he hasn't changed anything about the space since his grandma lived here with him six years ago.

He pulls me into his arms, and I tuck my head under his chin, resting my cheek against his chest. I close my eyes at the sound of his heart beating, tightening my arms around his waist to soak it all in.

"What sort of movie do you wanna watch?" He steps back, lifting my chin to look at him. "I'm up for anything as long as you don't force me to sit through all the lovey-dovey shit."

"I guess that's okay. I don't need you getting any ideas." His brow raises.

"I mean, you did say you didn't invite me over with ulterior motives. Are you saying you lied, Mr. Briggs?"

He traces the edge of my lip with his thumb, and I suck in a sharp breath, waiting for what he's about to say.

"If I did, do you think I could make it up to you with snacks?" he whispers.

A smile breaks out across my face, and he saunters toward the kitchen to grab a bag off the counter.

"I grabbed sour Skittles and gummy worms, just for you."

"Did you know to grab these, or is this pure luck?" I question.

I cross my arms over my chest, narrowing my gaze on him. He bends down to pick up the remote and begins scrolling through the movies. He stops on *Halloween*, then turns back toward me and nods toward the screen.

"The candy?" he asks absentmindedly.

I nod. "You picked up my favorites. How did you know?"

He looks guilty, like I just caught him in a lie. "I guess it was luck."

"Liar."

He presses his lips into a firm line, clicking the button to start the movie, and shrugs. "Okay, so maybe I've noticed you eating them a time or two. I picked them up earlier today."

"You really did plan this, didn't you?" I snicker. "Who would've thought Tysin could be sweet and plan a date?"

He narrows his eyes into a playful glare.

"Well, if you're trying to get in my pants, it's working." I snort.

"All because I invited you over for scary movies with some sour candy?" He stalks toward me, lifting me by my thighs into his arms.

I yelp, wrapping my arms around his neck to hold on, flinging the bag of candy onto the couch.

"Among other reasons." I shrug.

"Care to share?"

I drag my fingers through his hair, tugging on the strands, and he tilts his chin in the process. He sucks in a low hiss at the sharp pain, his eyes darkening on mine.

He drops down on the couch, still holding me in his arms, and the move leaves me straddling his lap. My hips rock against his, and he grits his teeth.

The familiar melody of the movie plays on low in the background, but neither of us pays any attention.

I drag my hand over his throat, gripping his chin. He tilts his mouth up, and I lean back, evading his mouth.

"Oh, so we're gonna play it that way, huh?" His large hands cover the curve of my ass, dragging me against him.

"You left me waiting for you to come around for a week. I think you deserve to be teased a little."

I lift my shirt over my head, leaving me dressed in my swimsuit top and shorts. Reaching for the bag of candy, I tear it open and pop a gummy worm into my mouth.

I roll my eyes closed and hum, sucking on the sour sugar before licking my finger.

Tysin's gaze burns into me, watching me enjoy the treat.

I reach into the bag for another and brush the sugar over my lips before dragging my tongue over them, sweeping the remnants from my mouth.

Tysin growls, watching me intently. I do the same to him, brushing the candy over his mouth before flicking my tongue over his lips to taste him.

"You and your fuckin' tongue." He grits his teeth. "I can't stop thinking about how good it's gonna feel when you wrap your lips around my dick and the sound of your moan when you taste my cum."

My breath hitches. He wraps his hand around my throat. Only this time, he doesn't let me pull back. His mouth crashes on mine, and I groan, letting him feel the vibration against his palm. His fingers tighten.

I blindly shove the candy back into the bag and toss it onto the couch, dragging my fingers through his hair to deepen the kiss.

This time when I pull the strands, he lifts his hips to thrust against me, and I grind my pussy over him, giving him back as much as he takes.

When I lean back from his mouth, he presses his forehead to mine and takes a deep breath.

"You make it so hard for me to keep my hands off you."

"What if I told you I wanted your hands all over me?"

He drags his hand down my chest and pauses over my heart, his eyes turning serious, and I'm waiting for what he's about to say. His finger brushes over the front of my swimsuit, and I wonder if he feels my heart hammering against his palm.

"Sin …" I trail off.

His eyes flicker, reaching his hand up to release my lip I hadn't realized I was biting.

I grip his wrist, turning my face into his hand, and kiss his palm before trailing to kiss his fingertips. They're rough and callused from years of playing guitar, but judging by his reaction when my lips meet his skin and he sucks in a breath, you'd never know it.

His eyelids lower, following each kiss starting with his pinky until I reach his pointer finger. He takes me off guard, tracing a line across my lower lip. I flick my tongue out to tease him, causing his nostrils to flare.

When I drag my tongue down the length of his finger, he lets out a low whistle, watching me intently as I do.

"You're playing a dangerous game."

He fidgets beneath me, and I smirk, fighting off the urge to let the smile take over my face.

If only he knew how much I loved the way his body reacted to me, he'd know I could do this all night.

"Goddamn, Kyla." He grunts when I suck his finger into my mouth.

He wiggles it when he reaches the back of my throat, and I open my mouth, letting him watch as I take him all.

"I promised you I didn't invite you over with other reasons in mind. If you keep this shit up, I'll be forced to break my promise."

I slowly drag his finger out, circling my tongue over the tip before trailing his hand down my chin and over my chest.

I stare down, watching his hand follow the path. I reach for the nylon material of my top, pulling it to the side to free my breast, and move his finger to circle the peak of my nipple.

He pulls back, this time sucking his finger into his mouth before brushing it over my puckered skin.

My whole body shudders, and I arch my back, grinding against him.

"Do it," I taunt him. "Break your promise, Tysin. For me."

We both know I mean this in more than one way.

It's not about tonight. It's more about him holding on to a promise he's made to himself not to give into me because of my brother.

I'd tempt him a million times if it meant seeing the haze of desire on his face.

"I can't wait to fuck your sweet little mouth."

His words come out more like a plea than a statement.

A slow smile stretches across my face, knowing I got him. I reach between us, gripping his hard length over his pants and cause him to hiss through his gritted teeth.

"Tell me you want me to stop."

I turn my hand over, rubbing my clit.

"Or do you want to make me beg?"

I stare at him beneath hooded eyes and recline back, giving him a better view. When he watches my hand slip inside my bikini bottoms, he gives in and unties the string knotted at my waist.

His gaze heats my skin, staring intently as my finger sinks into my pussy. His chest heaves before he tightens his hand around my wrist, lifting my fingers to his mouth.

He screws his eyes shut; the sound of his moan mixed with my name.

A niggling thought in the back of my mind warns me to be careful, to protect my heart. Tysin said it himself—we're playing a dangerous game.

I don't give a shit anymore. No matter what happens, I'll never be the same after tonight.

We always crave what we can't have.

CHAPTER SEVEN

KYLA

I wake to the sharp sound of lightning cracking nearby, followed by the low rumbling thunder. I lift my head from Tysin's bare chest, staring up at him and his arm resting above his head over the edge of the couch. Our legs are tangled together from when we fell asleep.

Tysin's long lashes fan out across the apples of his cheeks, his lips slightly parted, begging me to slide up and kiss him awake.

His eyes flutter, his chin jolting to the side. He winces, his brows deepening, and a low growl follows.

"No, you can't do that. You can't," he cries out.

He clenches his jaw, curling his lips in a snarl, and his nostrils flare with venom.

"I won't let you. You hear me? You can go to hell."

My heart rate spikes, pushing myself to my knees to lean over him.

"Tysin," I whisper, reaching out to shake him on the shoulder.

He grunts, shaking his head violently. I rear back, careful not to let him accidentally hit me in the process. I reach my hand out for his and lace our fingers.

"Tysin, baby, wake up." I clutch our folded hands against my chest and attempt to shake him, this time with more force than before.

Lightning flickers through the bay window, and the rain begins to pick up, pelting against the side of the house.

"You fuckin' bastard," Tysin hisses.

Not knowing what else to do, I crawl up his body and straddle his hips, leaning over to wrap my arms around his neck to hold him. His body thrashes beneath me, attempting to push me off before finally relaxing.

"Is everything okay?" he whispers, his breath heaving against my ear. He pushes my hair away from my face to look at me.

"You were having a bad dream. I didn't know how to wake you." I lean back enough to stare down at him.

His brow furrows, and for a second, I think he's going to tell me about it. His eyes soften, and he stares at my lips.

"I'm sorry if I scared you."

I tilt my head to the side. Why would he think he scared me?

He closes his eyes, his forehead wrinkling as if the memories plaguing him in his dreams were coming back to him, and the pain crashed into him like a wave in the storm.

"Tysin, you know if you ever need or want someone to talk to, you can always talk to me. Right?"

He slowly blinks his eyes open and nods. The change was so subtle that if I weren't soaking in every move and look on his face, I might've missed it.

My heart aches thinking about the source of the pain, memories of the anger-fueled words spewed at him full of hatred, and the young boy on the receiving end not understanding how someone who is supposed to love him could treat him the way she does.

I wish I could go back to those memories and wrap my arms around him and tell him not to believe his mother.

He sighs heavily and closes his eyes, and my chest tightens as the sorrow sweeps through me. I don't know how to break through the wall Tysin has built right before my eyes.

I slip my arms around him, pressing my body to his. He shudders beneath me, drawing in a sharp breath before his hands slowly brush over my sides and hold me to him.

"I love you, Tysin."

The words are out of my mouth before I have a chance to think them through. His body tenses, and I bite down on my lower lip, fighting off the urge to take the words back as the fear of rejection stings.

I don't, though, because regardless of the harsh reality of him not returning my feelings, I want him to know he deserves and is worthy of love.

"I don't remember the last time someone told me they loved me."

His voice cracks and I pull back, staring down at him just as another flash of lightning hits, illuminating the room.

Tears prick my eyes and my lip trembles. I release a slow breath, blinking through them, not wanting to let my emotions take hold of me. He's opening up, and I'm afraid if he sees it, it may force the wall he's slowly lowered for me back up. Words fail me when our eyes connect.

"Hey." He reaches his hand out, slipping it into my hair to pull me toward him. "Don't be upset. Please."

I shake my head, leaning into his palm, and let my eyes flutter closed. "I've loved you since I was a teenager. For as long as I've known you, Tysin. You deserve to know you're loved."

His throat bobs as he swallows, and I lean in, my mouth crashing down on his. He moans just before his tongue brushes against my lips. I open up to him, desperately needing more.

He sits up, and I follow him, tangling my arms around his neck to hold him to me. When he pulls back, breaking us apart, his eyes darken.

"Kyla"—he breathes harshly—"I'll never deserve you. I'm no good for you, and it's only a matter of time before I break your heart."

I shake my head. I don't believe him.

"You're wrong."

He chuckles. "Kyla—"

"Tysin, no. Even if you're right and you break my heart, it doesn't change how I feel about you. You may think you don't deserve to be loved. You may not believe me when I tell you I love you, but you're wrong."

His nostrils flare, and his chest heaves. He shakes his head, and the move grates against my nerves.

I grab his chin in my fingers, forcing him to look at me. "You're wrong."

"Then show me."

He grips my hips and moves to flip me on my back, pinning me against the couch. He reaches for my hands, holding them in one hand above my head. My legs are still wrapped around his waist, but I tighten my ankles around his back, forcing his body against me.

He squeezes his eyes shut, grinding his hips against my center, and I roll my eyes back, breathlessly whispering his name.

It's as if it were the permission he was waiting for, leaning in to attack my neck.

"I want you to fuck me ..." I beg. "Please."

I drag my fingers through his hair, holding him close to me. I grind my pussy against his hard length, feeling him through the thin material of his shorts.

He pulls back, reaching for the hem of my shirt. I sit up enough for him to pull it over my head, and he tosses it absentmindedly on the floor.

"Kyla," he moans, burying his face in my chest. He licks and nips at my skin, down my stomach to the waist of my shorts.

"Please," I moan, lifting my hips toward him.

"I will, baby."

He quickly pops the button and drags my shorts down, with my bottoms, in one swift move, leaving me spread open and bare for him.

His mouth drops open, and he releases a string of curse words at the sight of my pussy.

"So perfect," he groans, leaning in to kiss up my inner thigh until he stops at my center. He brushes his finger over my clit before dipping the tip inside my pussy.

"You're so fuckin' wet," he croaks. He almost sounds like he's in pain.

His fingers grip my thighs, pushing them against my chest to give him better access. When he flicks his tongue over my clit, I roll my eyes shut again, moaning out a loud, "Oh fuckkkk."

Those two words drive him wild, unleashing something deep and sinister inside him.

He leans back, adding a finger, and my pussy clenches hard around him.

"You like that, baby?" he grits out. "Your pussy loves my fingers. Just wait until I fuck this tight cunt."

I untie my top, freeing my breasts, and they bounce with each thrust of his hand. He curls his fingers, finding the delicious spot inside that drives me fucking crazy.

He alternates between flicking and rubbing his thumb over my clit. I can't seem to keep up. All the oxygen is sucked right out of me.

"Sin." My voice is low and sultry. "Please, I need more."

He quickly stands and sheds his shirt, then drops his shorts to the floor. His tattooed hand wraps around the length of his dick, and my mouth goes dry.

I fall to my knees on the floor in front of him, desperately wanting to taste him.

"My little sinner, on her knees for me." His lips curve in a devilish grin.

He grips my chin, bending forward to kiss me hard before standing.

"Open that sweet mouth."

Oh God, something about the way he talks dirty makes it hard not to beg him to take me every way he wants.

He brushes the tip along my lower lip, and I swipe my tongue over the sensitive flesh. He grits his teeth and moans, sliding inside my mouth slowly to test my limits.

"Look at me. I want to see your eyes when you take this dick."

When I reach my hands out, holding his thighs, urging him on, he tilts his head back and pistons his hips again. This time harder than the last.

"Sweetest fuckin' mouth," he hisses. "You look so fucking sexy with your lips around my cock."

I love hearing his praise, and this time when he thrusts back, I ready myself to take him deeper. When he slides into my mouth, I hold him, testing how much of him I can take.

His fingers grip my hair, pulling the strands as he holds on, and the muscles in his stomach clench.

"Holy shit, I'm gonna come. C'mere," he moans, pulling out.

He uses my spit to jerk off, and I climb up on the couch, staring at him as he fucks his fist. When he collapses onto the cushion next to me, I don't wait for his instruction.

Climbing over his lap, I position him at my entrance and slowly slide down his hard length. I toss my head back, and his fingers dig into my thighs, moaning and cursing my name.

I swivel my hips, wrapping my hand around his throat, and attack his mouth. I kiss him hard, biting and nipping at his lip.

He reaches his hand between us, brushing his thumb over my clit. This time, I force my pussy back down faster, taking him harder than before.

"Ride me, baby."

His nostrils flare, and his jaw clenches when I swivel my hips, taking all of him.

I want everything he has to give me.

I grip my breasts in my hands, flicking and tweaking my nipples with each brush of his finger over my clit.

"I want to feel you come around my dick."

Each thrust, each flick of his finger, brings me closer and closer to the edge. When he leans forward, wrapping his lips around my nipple, I feel the rush of my release, sending me catapulting over the edge.

"Ohh, fuck, baby," he groans, wrapping his arms around my waist to increase the force of his thrusts.

When I collapse against his chest, his breaths coming out in heavy pants, I slip my arms around his neck and bury my face in his neck.

A few minutes pass, long enough for our breathing to even out and our bodies to relax from our post-sex haze.

"No one has ever told me they love me, except my grandma."

Pulling back, I stare down at him, surprised by his admission.

No one, really? Not even his mom?

I guess I'm not surprised. The woman is downright awful, but my heart breaks for little Tysin going all his life never hearing her tell him she loves him.

"I've never said it to anyone out loud before either. Sometimes, I wonder if I even know what love feels like at all," he admits.

Tears prick my eyes for the brokenness in his depths. His face softens, and his throat bobs. I hold his cheeks in my hands, brushing my thumbs over his skin, and press a soft kiss against his lips.

Every day, from that day forward, when I spoke about love, I would measure it by how much I felt for Tysin. If only he knew how much he truly meant to me then.

CHAPTER EIGHT

TYSIN

Whiskey Barrel is packed wall to wall. We slip in through the employee entrance, bypassing the line forming out the front door and roping around the side of the building.

Music booms through the speakers blaring Three Days Grace. I peek my head through the door leading to the back room, scanning over the crowd holding their drinks and phones in the air, swaying as they sing along to the lyrics.

I untwist the cap of my beer, lifting it to my lips, and take a swig when I spot Kyla amongst the crowd sitting at a table with a few of her friends I recognize. She lifts her hand in the air, waving over to Ivy for another round of drinks. Her lavender hair stands out in the sea of people.

I haven't seen her in a few days, not since the night she stayed over. I've thought a lot about where this is going ever since that night.

The tension and attraction have been slowly building for years.

My loyalty is to my best friend. The last thing I want is to interfere with our friendship, but I've fought my feelings for Kyla for far too long.

Everything changed between us the night she said she loved me.

I never expected it, and I certainly wasn't ready for things to change. Especially when I knew in my heart I couldn't be the man she deserved.

I knew it, Madden knew it, and I wrestled with the thought of how to break it to her too.

I swallow the guilt with my heavy swig of beer, hating the fact I've taken the coward's way out. I've kept my distance from her, knowing the more I'm around her, the more difficult it's become for me to give in to the temptation.

She has me all twisted in knots, and even though I can't admit it out loud, it's true.

We claim one of the high-top tables, and the crowd parts as Brix makes his way toward where Madden and I are sitting, shooting the shit before we hit the stage. He's like fucking royalty around here. People bow down to him, giving him space to get through until he reaches us. Maybe because he is around this town. His dad is loaded, and he's never had to want for anything his whole life.

"Things are getting serious between the two of you, huh?" Madden asks, nodding toward the bar where Brix came from. He lifts his beer and takes a drink to put off answering the question.

His voice comes out hoarse and grumbly. Brix shrugs, climbing onto the barstool across from us.

"I hate to break it to you, but it looks like it's her who has you eating out of the palm of her hand!" I holler over the music, chuckling.

"Shut the fuck up," Brix grits out.

"Well, looks like you've won part of the bet. You fucked her." Madden elbows me at the mention of the bet, glancing around for any sign of Ivy. I clutch my side, gritting my teeth. "I'm waiting for the part where you send her ass heartbroken back to wherever the hell she came from, though."

"I said shut the fuck up, you stupid motherfucker. You hear me?" Brix seethes. "You have a lot of room to talk when you've been keeping secrets of your own."

He bores his eyes into me, clenching his jaw as if signaling to test him on it.

"Hey guys, you ready to rock this place or what?" Kyla's sweet voice yells over the music.

My eyes stay glued on Brix.

"Will you two knock it the fuck off?" Madden shouts. "I'm sick of you constantly bickering like teenage girls. We have a show to play, and we don't need you at each other's throats, all right?"

"I'm gonna go warm up," I growl, swallowing the rest of my beer and slamming the bottle down on the table.

I don't doubt for a second that Brix would spill my secret about seeing Kyla behind Madden's back, but he wouldn't do it right before we have a show to play.

"Wait, Tysin, what's wrong?" Kyla asks under her breath. Her eyes flick over to Madden, not wanting to cause a scene.

"Listen, I can't talk to you right now. I don't want to deal with your brother and Brix and their shit-ass mood."

She clenches her jaw and nods, taking a step back.

There's a glimmer in her eyes, looking an awful lot like tears, but she blinks through them, not letting it show.

I hate the thought of hurting her. It's the last thing I want. I'm no better than Brix, which is precisely why Madden would never condone me dating his sister.

He knows all about my sordid past and the long list of women I've taken home before her. She's nothing like them, though, but it doesn't matter. He'd never see it that way.

Madden is protective over Kyla. I'd never want a girl to get between the band and me, and the future we've mapped out for us.

I stalk away from her, unable to bear the look in her eyes anymore.

A line of women forms along the stage, and as soon as they see me approaching, their attention is on me.

I recognize one of them right away.

Victoria.

We hooked up once months ago. She knew the score and was up for a good time with no strings attached.

"Hey," she coos when I approach, dragging her hand over my chest.

I stare down at her long nails, recalling the way she dragged them over my back, digging into my skin.

It was the most delicious pain.

"You want another beer before you go on?" Oaklyn, one of the bartenders, interrupts to ask. She flicks her eyes over to Victoria, curling her lip in disgust before looking back at me.

Oaklyn smirks.

"I'll take another, please." I hold my finger up.

She nods, turning and disappearing through the crowd.

I shoulder past Victoria to where our equipment is set up near the stage. I reach for my guitar and lift the strap over my head, adjusting it under my arm. I grip the pick in my fingers, flicking the strings.

The sound of the guitar plays around the room, garnering some attention. When I glance up, it's as if my body is in tune with where she is, and my eyes meet Kyla's.

She's sitting at the table across from Madden, joining him and Brix. She breaks my eye contact when she notices me look in her direction, glancing down at something on the table in front of her.

She must've spotted me talking to Victoria.

"What are you doing later tonight?" Victoria coos.

"No idea," I grunt, adjusting the tuning peg and plucking the string to check the sound.

Her hand brushes over my forearm and up my shoulder, and my eyes follow her move before flashing over to her.

She bats her eyelashes at me seductively. I spot Brix behind her approaching.

I nod. "Stick around after the show, and maybe I'll take you up on it."

Her face beams, a grin taking over, and she bounces on her feet. "I'll be right here."

"You know, for as much shit as you talk about me with Ivy, you don't have any room to talk about how you treat Kyla," Brix growls.

"What in the hell are you talking about? You don't know shit about my relationship with Kyla."

"I don't?" He smirks. His lip curls on the edge, and it grates on my nerves.

"Nah, man, you don't know shit." I snarl, following him into the back room away from the crowd.

"You don't think she talks to Ivy and hasn't brought it up to me?"

I narrow my eyes on him. "What did she say?"

"Listen, this is my final warning. You stay the fuck out of my relationship with Ivy, and I'll stay out of yours."

I put my hands up. There's an anger in his voice I haven't heard before, and I concede. It's not worth ruining our friendship over anyway.

"I'm not gonna tell you what to do when it comes to Kyla. You're a big fuckin' boy and can take care of yourself. I'll warn you, though. If Madden finds out about you fuckin' his sister and then turning around bringing groupies home with you, he's going to wring your ass out to dry."

"Chill the fuck out, will ya?"

Brix chuckles, shaking his head. "I'm just sayin', we both know how much loyalty means to him. He's loyal to you and the band, but all that will fly out the fuckin' window when he figures out you're mistreating his sister."

"All right, I fuckin' hear you. Dear God. Are you sure you're gettin' laid? I swear, something's got your panties in a wad. Why don't you call Ivy back here and ask her for a hand?"

He rolls his eyes, stalking behind me and back into the bar.

We take the stage not long after, and as always, the packed crowd at Whiskey Barrel doesn't disappoint. Although Brix doesn't get into it like he used to, gyrating and feeding into the wild fans lining the front of the stage, they give it right back to him.

Madden starts us off on drums, and I follow him on the bass guitar, nodding my head in time to the beat.

I stare at the crowd, the row of women lining the front of the stage clamoring for a chance to touch me. The humidity in the bar is so thick, leaving beads of sweat dotting my brow.

Our set ends in a crescendo of drums and guitar riffs. Brix jumps off the stage into the crowd as they chant and beg for more. Adrenaline races through my body. If it weren't for wanting to give my wrist and fingers a break, I'd go all night.

It's after midnight when we wrap up. I'm ready to grab another cold one and relax. A brunette across the bar seems to capture Madden's attention, so when Kyla approaches me, he doesn't notice us talking.

"You got plans tonight?" she asks, glancing over at Madden to see if he's looking.

"I'm gonna call it an early night."

She winces, the pang of rejection evident on her face before she quickly smoothes it over.

"I'll see ya around, Tysin." She shakes her head.

"Kyla." She stops in her tracks, peering back over at me.

"I'll hit you up when I get home, all right?"

She flicks her eyes over to Madden, then looks around to see if anyone is listening before focusing on me.

"Listen, I don't know what's gotten into you tonight, but I'm not going to stand here and watch you flirt with other women and take them home, then come back to me when you're bored. It's not gonna fuckin' happen."

"Now is not a good time to talk about this."

"I've said what I want to say on the matter. I won't let you treat me like I'm some backup plan or a second choice." She snaps her mouth shut, the emotion burning in her eyes.

"Kyla—"

She holds her hand up to stop me. "I haven't spoken to you in days, Tysin. I know we haven't talked about what's going on between us, but you need to figure out what you want. Or I'll be the one to figure it out for us both."

CHAPTER NINE

KYLA

I wanted to believe it was all in my head.

"I swear I'm never dating another man for as long as I live," I grumble, collapsing on my bed.

I quickly changed into my pajamas as soon as I got home, my hair tied into a knot. The weight of exhaustion settles over me, but the sinking feeling in the pit of my stomach says I won't be able to sleep tonight. Foo Fighters plays in the background, helping drown out the thoughts hitting me one after another.

I attempt to focus on the lyrics, absentmindedly scrolling TikTok to occupy my mind. All I've been able to think about is how different things seemed to be with Tysin tonight at Whiskey Barrel.

He was on edge, distant, and didn't seem to pay attention at all to the fact I was there. The same thing happened with Ivy. Even though she insisted she didn't feel well, I couldn't figure it out.

When the band wrapped up their set, I waited for Tysin to signal for me to meet him at his place. Things were perfect the last night we spent together. I wanted to believe there was something else going on.

I try justifying in my mind that maybe he got into an argument with his mom again, or maybe he was not getting along with the guys before their show? He's been working on his motorcycle for weeks. What if something happened with his bike?

I was using anything to justify the distance between us. I couldn't cover up the feeling churning in my stomach. Something was going on.

It has nothing to do with his mom, the band, or his bike. None of it. It's all about me, us.

My phone vibrates in my hand, and Ivy's name flashes on the screen. I glance over at the nightstand, the time just after two in the morning.

Why would she be calling so late?

"Hey," I answer. I'm met with the sound of a heart-aching sob filtering through the phone.

I sit up quickly, pressing the phone firmly to my cheek. "Ivy, what's wrong? Are you okay? Did something happen?" I rattle off.

"Can I stop over?"

My parents are out of town for their annual weekend trip to Raleigh. They grew up there and make the drive every summer for their anniversary. It left me home in the quiet house, taking care of our dogs.

"Of course, I'm home. I'll see you in a few."

She ends the call with a breathy goodbye. I jog down the stairs and unlock the door, peeking through the side window until the small headlights of Ivy's old beat-up car pull in behind mine.

I flick on the front porch light, and as soon as I see the look on her face, I know whatever she's about to tell me won't be good.

"What happened? Are you okay?" I ask, holding the door open for her.

Her eyes are puffy and red, remnants of mascara stream down her face, and her hair is pulled up in a bun matching my own. She's dressed in shorts and a sweatshirt; the temperature has dropped since earlier in the night.

"I want to say goodbye to you before I go."

"Go? Go where? Where are you going?"

She stares down at the floor, shaking her head. I reach for her hand, tugging her with me into the living room, and gesture for her to sit on the couch.

"Let me get you some water, okay? Give me just a second."

She nods, and I escape into the kitchen to grab her a bottle of water and some ibuprofen. She looks like she's been crying her eyes out, and I have no doubt she'll be fighting off a headache before too long.

Give me a chance to say I'm sorry.

The familiar lyrics break through the silence when I walk back into the living room. Ivy's seated on the couch, staring down at her phone. The music playing came from her phone.

"I'm sorry. I hope I didn't wake anyone. I didn't realize my ringer was on."

"I'm the only one home. My parents are out of town for the weekend."

She sighs, her phone flashing again, and she shakes her head. "It's Brix." She hits the power button, turning it off. "He won't stop calling if he's noticed I'm gone."

"Did something happen between the two of you?"

I take a seat on the edge of the sofa next to her. She releases a shuddered breath, waving her hands around while searching for the words but can't seem to find the answers.

"I'm not ready to talk about it. Not yet. All I know and can say is whatever relationship I thought we were building was never real to him. It was all a bet between him and Tysin. We're nothing more than a joke."

My heart aches for my friend, but the mention of it being a bet, a joke, between him and Tysin causes my stomach to drop.

"Promise me you'll be careful with him," Ivy says.

"Did he say anything about me? Where did you hear this?"

"From their own mouths. I don't know about your relationship, though. I didn't stay long enough to hear the rest of the conversation. I could barely hold myself together."

"Is this why you weren't feeling well tonight?"

She nods. "I didn't know what to say or do."

She struggles to finish the sentence. For me, it's like I've been sucker punched. Tears prick my eyes. I'm trying to be there for my friend, but my heart feels like it's breaking inside my chest.

I told him I loved him, and he never returned the feelings.

What if I was nothing but a joke to him too?

A conquest.

Would he really do something like this to his best friend's sister?

Who was the Tysin I've spent time with and got to know?

"There's only a couple of weeks left before school starts. I called my friend Hensley, and she's agreed to let me stay with her until we can get into our dorm. I'm heading back to Chapel Hill tonight."

"Right now?" I ask.

We still have so much planned before the end of the summer. I hate the thought of my best friend leaving so fast when we both need each other.

In the end, I know it'll be too hard to stay in Carolina Beach when she's forced to live in the same house as Brix. I try to convince her to stay with me even for the night, but she declines, wanting to get the drive over with since she won't be able to sleep.

She stays a few more minutes, thanking me for the ibuprofen and water. Before she takes off, we make plans for me to visit her soon so we can hit up their nightclubs and check out some upcoming concerts in the area.

I toss and turn all night, unable to fall asleep. It wasn't until almost four in the morning when I finally succumbed to exhaustion, and sleep pulled me under. It's short-lived, though, because when pounding on the door wakes me, I find a disheveled Brix standing at my door.

I've never seen Brix like this. You'd think he got hit by a semi. His shirt is wrinkled like he plucked it off the floor and pulled it on with his denim jeans. His boots are untied as if he shoved his feet into them and couldn't be bothered with lacing them before taking off to my house.

"Is she here?" he asks. His voice twists in pain, cracking on the word she.

"Awfully brave of you to come over here alone."

"Kyla, please. I need to talk to her."

"You don't deserve to speak to her ever again."

"What did she tell you?"

"Something about a bet between you and Tysin. Is that all we were to you two? Some bet?"

"What?! No, it had nothing to do with you. I swear. It was stupid, okay? He was razzing me the night she came into town after she rejected me. He thought it was hilarious that she wanted nothing to do with me after I hit on her."

"So, what? You made a bet with him to prove you could get with her? You're a fuckin' prick, Brix. You know that?"

"I know, okay? I don't deserve her, but you need to help me find her. I need a chance to talk to her, to explain everything."

"It's too late."

His face drops, and he shakes his head. "What do you mean it's too late?"

"She left. She went back to school. It's over. She's gone."

He drags his hands through his hair, pacing back and forth across my porch before bending over. He drops his head between his shoulders, his body trembling with emotion.

I almost feel bad for him for a second, but I shove the thought out of my mind.

"Why did you do this in the first place? If you're so upset about her leaving, why put yourself in the position to lose her at all?"

"I didn't expect to fall in love with her, Kyla."

He stands, his hair sticking up on top. I suspect this isn't the first time he's run his hands through his hair in frustration.

"It still doesn't answer the question. Why would you do this to her, Brix?"

"I wasn't thinking at the time. If I could go back to that night, don't you think I'd tell Tysin to take his bullshit comments and shove them up his ass? I was pissed off, and she hated me, and it killed me to see how unaffected she was around me."

I snicker. "The arrogant and self-centered Brix finally gets a taste of his own medicine."

He swallows hard, his throat bobbing, and he nods. "I guess you're right."

"Why didn't you come clean to her before she found out?"

"I wanted to, Kyla. I tried, trust me, I tried. How do you tell someone you love a secret you've kept from them when you know it'll crush them and ruin everything?"

He had a point. As hard as it would be to tell her, he had to know he risked losing her once he did.

"It looks like you already did," I say. Stepping back into the house, I let the screen door slam shut behind me.

Brix reaches for the door handle, quick to try to stop me.

"Please, wait."

"What the hell do you want from me? I told you; she's gone."

"Will you please call her? Talk to her, convince her to give me a chance to explain."

"No."

"No? Why?"

"I'm not certain you deserve a chance to explain, Brix. Even if you did, it's her decision, and I'm not going to convince her of anything. If you want to prove you're sorry, you'll have to go about it a different way. Because it won't be through me."

He squeezes his eyes shut and tilts his head back, accepting defeat.

"Hey, Brix," I say, just before I shut the door.

He gazes back down at me.

I hate to kick a man when he's down, but my loyalty isn't to him. It's to Ivy.

"You're an asshole." I raise my middle finger in the air and slam the door in his face.

CHAPTER TEN

KYLA

Everything has turned to shit.

Brix hasn't stopped blowing up my phone incessantly about Ivy.

She refuses to speak with him, and rightfully so, but he's going out of his mind. He's holding out hope I'll give in and relay a message to her for him.

It's no secret there was animosity between Brix and Ivy when she first came into town. He was her childhood enemy turned stepbrother. The hatred between them was enough to fuel a freight train.

No one expected him to bet he could make her fall in love with him, only to break her heart. He hadn't expected to fall in love with her in the process.

To top it all off, I'm on day five of no word from Tysin. Every one of my texts and calls have gone unanswered, taking the knife and twisting it deeper and deeper.

I've lain in bed every night staring at the same picture hanging on the wall in my bedroom, the anxiety eating away at me. Why couldn't Tysin talk to me? All I wanted was for him to say something, anything to put to rest all the thoughts racing through my mind.

The stifling humidity hangs thick in the air. I stare blankly at the television, listening to the meteorologist drone on about a storm rolling up the Eastern Seaboard. Carolina Beach was expected to get hit hard.

If the weather was any indication, I should've listened to the bad feeling twisting in my stomach about what was to come, but I didn't let it stop me.

Word had gotten around about a party Tysin was throwing at his place. I have to get to the bottom of things and figure out what's going on between us. I just hope it won't end up where I fear this is going.

I don't bother turning on any music on the drive over to Tysin's. Instead, I imagine what I could be walking into, picturing the look on his face when he first sees me.

I replay everything I want to say to him, praying this is all a big misunderstanding.

A line of cars leads from the front of his house, wrapping around the corner of the block. Music blares, reverberating through the house so loud you can hear it from where I parked across the street. People spill out onto the patio, stumbling and standing in small groups smoking cigarettes with beers in their hands. Bottles and cans litter the front yard, and I begin to wonder if he's had this same party more than once this week.

My eyes flash to the dashboard, the time on the clock reading 11:11. My chest seizes, recognizing the significance before taking a quick look in the rearview mirror.

I drag my fingers through my dark chocolate-brown hair. I decided on a whim to make a change, dying it myself from the lavender color I've rocked for years. I glance down at the deep purple and black lace corset I'm wearing and the choker around my neck.

If I'm walking in here to get my heart broken, I want him to know exactly what he's losing.

I search the rows of cars for any sign of Madden's, but it's nowhere in sight. It doesn't mean he's not around somewhere. Hell, he can show up at any minute.

This is my chance to get Tysin alone, and I have to take it.

I release a heavy exhale, trying to muster up the courage to walk into his house. I want to get this over with, so I push myself up his driveway, the sound of my high heels clicking on the concrete.

I recognize a few people from high school and nights at Whiskey Barrel.

When I step into the kitchen through the side door, red cups and pizza boxes are stacked on the counter. It's packed to the brim with people pouring rows of shots and mixed drinks. A group of guys huddles around the dining table, yelling and cheering over an intense game of flip cup.

I weave my way through people, searching for any sign of Tysin.

Of all the scenarios I've run through in my mind on the drive over, I know I made a mistake the moment I turn the corner into the living room.

I would give anything to turn around, climb back in my car, and drive myself far away from here. The pain slicing through my heart feels like everything I ever wanted was ripped out of my hands all at once.

Tears form in my eyes, staring at Tysin reclined back on his sofa. The same one we spent the night together on. A brunette straddles his lap and leans back, thrusting her chest into his face. He reaches out, gripping her breast in his hand, smiling in appreciation. The bleach-bottle blonde next to him kisses her way up his neck, dragging her fingers through his hair.

Like some sort of masochist, I can't bring myself to tear my eyes away.

In a matter of seconds, my heart is crushed in the palm of his hand.

The two girls turn to each other, their tongues dueling in a kiss. In the midst of their heated moment, Tysin's gaze flashes beyond them and meets mine.

He pushes the brunette off his lap and stumbles to his feet, stalking toward me. His footsteps falter when the crowd parts, getting a good look at me. His eyes trail slowly over my body, glazed and hungry, eating up every inch.

When he takes another step toward me, I quickly turn to leave. I need to get out of here. I thought I wanted to do this, but I can't. Not after what I just witnessed.

If it's all a joke or some bet, and all he wants is to hurt me, then fine. He's won.

I try to weave through the crowd of people, but it's so packed it's impossible to make a fast exit. I glance over my shoulder when I feel his strong hand reach out and grip my arm to stop me.

"Come with me."

His voice is loud and angry. How the fuck is he mad at me when it's his fault we are in this position?

"C'mon," he hollers, nodding his head down the hallway toward his bedroom.

He doesn't let me go, sliding his hand down my forearm and lacing his fingers in mine to tug me with him. He grabs a set of keys from his pocket and shoves one into the lock. He opens the door and pulls me with him inside, slamming it behind us.

I take a step away from him, forcing my back against the wall.

The light on his nightstand is on, but it's faint, hardly doing enough to light the dark space. It's still enough to make out the look on his face.

He's livid, and I don't understand why.

"You want to tell me what the hell I just walked into, Tysin?"

It takes everything in me not to let the emotions swallow me whole.

He narrows his eyes, shaking his head as if he can't believe I'm even asking the question.

"You know what? No, never mind." I reach for the door handle, but he pushes past me, slamming the door shut again. "I guess you made your choice, huh? This is what you want."

"You should've known what you would be walking into when you showed up here unannounced."

I whip my head back toward him. "Excuse me? So it's okay for you to show up at my work when you want to see me, but when you've blown me off for days and I hear you're having a party, it's not okay for me to do the same?"

His nostrils flare, and he shakes his head.

"There's no point in having this conversation with you, Tysin. I shouldn't have even come over. I'm done. Do you hear me? I'm done."

"I don't know what you thought was going on between us, but it's not what you think," he growls.

My mouth drops open, unable to form words.

He pushes his thumb and finger against the corner of his eyes, squeezing them shut.

"You should've listened to me the first time I told you I'd only break your heart."

My heart drops to the pit of my stomach.

"You deserve more than I could ever give you," he adds.

"Famous last words. You sound like a coward right now."

He winces and nods. A part of me believes this is what he wanted, to push me so far away only to prove he isn't worthy of being loved.

His eyes burn into my face, taking in the change in my hair, trailing down my body. He sucks in a breath when he stops on my corset, clenching his jaw before swallowing hard when he meets my gaze once more.

I turn toward the door and take a deep breath before reaching for the handle.

"Don't go. Not yet," he says, reaching his hand out to grip my hips.

He pulls me back against him, and I hate my traitorous body for melting into his.

"Why? You already have what you want waiting for you out there."

He sighs heavily, pressing his forehead against my shoulder. "You have no idea what you're talking about."

"I don't? I know what I saw when I walked in here. Not one, but two women, Tysin."

"They're not you."

I spin around, pushing him to step back in the process.

"That's them, and you're you. No one could ever be you," he growls.

Just like that, my heart breaks all over again.

He grips my chin between his fingers, capturing me in a hard, punishing kiss. I slip my hands into his hair, my nails raking over his scalp, and pull on the strands.

He hisses, tilting his head back, and moans.

"Is that what you want, Kyla?" His nostrils flare. "You want me to fuck you one last time and ruin me for all others?"

"Shut up," I grit out.

He leans down, his lip curving in a grin.

"I've always loved the fire in you."

He runs his hand over my chest, cupping my breast through my corset top, before venturing farther to wrap around my throat. I tilt my head back against the wall.

"What if I want to ruin you for every other man too?"

I shake my head. Doesn't he understand he already has? He's destroyed me.

"I hate you," I spit out. "I hate you for what you've done to me."

There's a flicker in his eye. Good. I hope the words landed like a strong punch to the gut.

He turns me in his arms and pushes my chest against the wall. He slips his hand over my front, nipping and plucking my nipple before sliding into the front of my pants.

My knees go weak, and I reach up to grip his forearm to steady myself.

He hums in appreciation when his fingers find their way into my panties, brushing over my clit.

"I don't believe you. Try again. Only this time, say it with more conviction."

I flare my nostrils. When he circles my clit, I dig my nails into his arm, screwing my eyes shut.

"Doesn't feel like you hate me." He snickers. "Always so wet for me. Your pussy knows who it belongs to, doesn't it, Kyla?"

"I said shut up," I say, punctuating every word.

He chuckles. My head drops back against his chest, and my legs nearly buckle beneath me.

I reach my hand behind me, gripping his dick through his pants, earning me a low growl.

"Always hungry for my dick, too. Ain't that right, baby?"

He pulls my hips toward him, taking a step back, and slides his hand down my spine, urging me to bend forward.

I brace my hands against the wall. He reaches around, unbuttoning my pants, and tugs them down my legs.

I'm left bare and exposed for him. His hands massage my ass cheeks, spreading them open before slapping one hard with a loud smack.

I hear the familiar sound of his belt unhooking, followed by his jeans dropping to the hardwood floor. I squeeze my eyes shut when his fingers brush through my pussy from behind. I sidestep, widening my stance, and moan when he shoves two fingers inside me.

He drops to his knees and groans appreciatively, spreading my ass cheeks open again. When his tongue flicks through my pussy, I desperately search for something to hold on to, feeling unsteady on my feet.

He pulls back again, brushing his finger through my folds before sliding deep inside me.

"Tell me how bad you want me," he grunts. "Let me hear you beg me to fuck you."

I want to tell him to shut up, but I'm afraid if I do, he'll stop. I want him too damn bad right now to risk him pulling back.

"Tysin," I mutter. "Please."

I grind my ass against him, and he quickly replaces his fingers with the tip of his dick. He brushes the head over my clit, lining up at my entrance when I thrust back into him, taking him hard and fast.

He fires out a stream of curse words, gripping my hips to pin me against him. His hand twists in my hair, and I suck in a sharp breath when he pulls on the strands, using it to tilt my head back toward him.

"Does that feel good?"

"Shut up and fuck me."

"My fuckin' pleasure," he growls just before he slams back into me. Each thrust is punctuated, hitting the right spot.

"I'm gonna miss this sweet pussy," he groans. "It's gonna ruin me."

"Tysin," I moan as tears fill my eyes.

My nails dig into the doorframe, trying desperately to hold on as he fucks me with everything he has, my feet wobbling in my heels.

"I'm close," he mutters against my ear. "Touch your pussy, baby. I want you to come with me."

I obey his orders, reaching my fingers between my legs. I rub my clit in circles, bracing my other hand against the wall, his thrusts hard and punishing.

He bites and nips at my neck. I moan loudly, rubbing my tight bud until my body shudders, and he follows close behind. His groans turn muffled against my ear as he breathlessly mutters my name.

I squeeze my eyes shut, knowing the sound of his voice will forever be ingrained in my memory.

He pulls out and stumbles back, leaning against the edge of his bed.

I glance over my shoulder, and he smiles, brushing his finger over his lip. The look in his eyes is hungry as if he needs a couple of minutes before he'll be ready for round two.

That's the thing about men like Tysin.

All they do is take, take, take without the intention of giving you anything back in return.

He's taken everything from me. I wince, shaking my head, feeling like a fool for giving in to him again.

I reach down, quickly pulling my jeans and panties over my hips. Running my fingers through my hair, I attempt to fix my appearance. It dawns on me it's possible I could run into my brother during my escape. The last thing I'd want is for him to see me freshly fucked, stomping out of his best friend's room.

"Where are you goin'?" Tysin asks, stopping me again as I reach for the door. "You don't have to leave, ya know. You can stay here tonight."

I stare down at my hand, tempted to open the door and walk out, not giving him the satisfaction of another word.

I can't, though, because no matter how much he's hurt me, I'm not him. I couldn't leave here without saying anything more to him.

I turn, leaning my back against the door. The wood cools my heated skin.

"I'm leaving, Tysin. When I walk out this door, this won't ever happen again."

His face goes blank, his jaw set. A part of me hopes he'll fight me on it, that he'll apologize and tell me he never wanted to hurt me.

Yet he doesn't say a word. He leans down, pulls up his jeans, and adjusts the belt at his waist before buckling it. He sheds his shirt, using the material to wipe the sweat from his face, tossing it into a hamper at the end of his bed.

He plucks a shirt out of the closet, quickly slips it over his head, and then looks back at me. His lip curls as he looks me up and down and nods.

"Then go."

I steel my spine and narrow my eyes on him, letting him feel the anger rolling off me in waves.

"You're Madden's best friend, so it's impossible to expect I'll never run into you again. Stay away from me. You hear me? You warned me you'd break my heart, and it turns out you were right. I never want to see you again."

"You done yet?" he quips.

I suck in a sharp breath, my nostrils flaring, and I shake my head. I reach for the door handle and stop, turning to look at him one last time.

"I hate you. I wish I never fell in love with you."

Do you want more of Tysin and Kyla's?

If you enjoyed Sins of a Rebel and want more of Tysin and Kyla's love story, keep reading to get a glimpse into

TYSIN! It's a steamy and forbidden brother's best friend, close proximity rock star romance.

Please consider also spreading the word and telling a friend or two. Word of mouth recommendations and reviews help readers find books! I'd appreciate if you left a review on Amazon, Bookbub or Goodreads. Thank you!

TYSIN

BOOK TWO

USA TODAY BESTSELLING AUTHOR
BROOKE O'BRIEN

CHAPTER ONE

KYLA

Of course, of all places, he wants to go to Whiskey Barrel.

I puff my lips out and release a slow exhale. Rain trickles down the window, my breath fogging the glass. A lump I've been struggling to swallow is forming in my throat.

The news reported a tropical storm hitting the East Coast, but we're only expecting to get hit with the outer bands. It's symbolic of the absolute hell of a week I've endured with finals consuming my life.

I've graduated with my college degree, so my father can finally get off my back.

He gave up on riding my older brother, Madden, a long time ago. I guess when your son is the drummer for one of the biggest rock bands on the radio, you start to let shit slide.

Warm skin brushes over my thigh, and I shift my gaze over to Canon. He tangles our fingers together, lifting our joined hands to press a soft kiss against the back of mine.

A pair of black Ray-Bans hides his eyes, despite the sun being nowhere in sight.

My gaze snaps down to his mouth when he drags his lip between his teeth. He's dressed in a black T-shirt and denim jeans, fitting him perfectly in all the right ways. His tattooed arm is stretched out, his tanned hand firmly gripping the steering wheel. He looks every bit of the rugged badass your parents want you to stay far away from.

Except my parents love him, even if it's only because of his last name.

"It's a Friday night. Wouldn't you rather take me back to your place and fuck me against the wall?"

He slides his sunglasses off and curls the edge of his lip in a smirk. His eyes narrow, and for a second, I think I may have got to him.

He whips the car into a spot in the parking lot. He reaches for the lever to the door, then glances back before pushing it open and stepping outside.

"Dammit." I huff.

My heart drops to the pit of my stomach as the door shuts. Not because of the rejection.

It's the last thing I'd ever expect from Canon. He's never given me a reason to doubt him or his love for me since we started dating last summer.

No, the twist in my stomach has everything to do with the fact I'm only a few minutes away from seeing Tysin.

Tysin Briggs is the biggest player in Carolina Beach and a recipe for heartbreak. Yet it didn't stop me from falling in love with him two years ago. The rush and the high were intoxicating, but the crash coming down left me broken in a million pieces.

The day I walked out of the hospital, I vowed to stay as far away from him as I could. We've managed to avoid each other, but I knew this day would come sooner or later.

He's my brother's best friend and bandmate. We live in the same small town. Whiskey Barrel was his hangout, where the band started out playing all their shows.

There would be no avoiding him here.

It wasn't until Canon came along that I finally began putting the pieces of my heart back together.

My relationship with Tysin, if you could even call it one, was always kept a secret. Somehow, that made it even harder to move on.

If it weren't for the memories that haunted me and the ache in my chest, I would've thought it was all a dream.

"You comin' or what?" Canon teases, snapping me from my thoughts when he opens my door.

I climb out, stepping to the side to let him close the door before he stops me, pushing me against the side of the car.

All the stress and anxiety melt away when he pulls me into him, and I slip my arms around his waist. He trails his lips from my temple, where he presses a kiss, down to my ear.

"Let's have some fun tonight, yeah? I mean, you did just graduate from college. You should be fuckin' excited, baby. You did it!"

Guilt pangs in my chest. Why am I letting thoughts of running into Tysin ruin my night when I have Canon right in front of me?

"I always have fun when I'm with you."

He grins, tilting his forehead against mine, and kisses me deeply. I slide my fingers over his chest and pull him down, gripping the back of his neck to hold him to me. He moans, the move vibrating against my hand.

"Let's go have some fun. You deserve it."

He reaches for my hand, lacing our fingers together while we walk through the parking lot. There's a shift in my mood, a noticeable weight lifting from my chest as we round the corner toward the bar. A long line wraps around the front of the building, which only happens on the nights when A Rebels Havoc plays.

"Isn't that Tysin?" Canon asks, motioning toward the side of the building.

I follow his line of sight, my eyes immediately locking on Tysin. He's leaning against the wall, his foot tucked under him.

So much has changed since the last time I saw him. Even the way he stares at me now. The once heated look of desire is now replaced with a bitter coldness.

I know, without a doubt, he sees me, his eyes falling on where our hands are linked together.

I grit my teeth, knowing it won't be as easy to avoid him as I hoped.

He lifts his cigarette to his mouth, taking a deep inhale. His eyes eventually drag from me over to Canon before releasing a slow puff of smoke.

He's wearing a pair of black denim jeans and a red T-shirt with matching scuffed-up Vans.

I hate him for how deliciously sexy he still is, even after all this time.

It dawns on me that Canon asked me a question. Turning to find his eyes burning into the side of my face, I nod, responding with a clipped, "Yep."

When I turn my gaze forward, I notice Tysin's eyes are back on me, slowly raking over my body.

The bouncer near the front recognizes me and nods, waving me past him.

"Didn't expect to see you tonight." Tysin's deep voice grumbles as we pass by. "I thought I ran you out of here a long time ago."

My footsteps falter, and it takes everything in me not to give him a piece of my mind. It's what he wants, though. If I let him get under my skin, and he knew how much it bothers me, we'd be back to the same old cat and mouse games he likes to play.

"What was that about?" Canon questions. He looks at me, then back over at him, his brows deepening in confusion.

"Who knows?" I reply, trying to brush him off.

Meanwhile, the lump forming in my throat grows, making it impossible to ignore.

Whiskey Barrel is packed wall to wall with people. I overhear one of the bouncers tell Canon they've hit capacity, meaning they can't let anyone else enter. Carolina Beach has always turned up for their hometown heroes, and to this town, the guys of A Rebels Havoc are like gods.

It's exactly why I want to get out of here.

Canon's hand finds mine again as we make our way through the crowd of people toward the bar. The band always reserves the first couple of tables near the front. They loved the attention they got here and liked being able to mingle with the crowd.

The farther we get inside, I'm able to spot Brix and Ivy standing near the stage, and Madden isn't too far from them. He's built like a linebacker and is impossible to miss.

When we were in high school, the coaches didn't stop hounding him to join the team. He never had any interest in sports. At least not playing. His passion has always been music. Even when we were younger, he would turn anything and everything into a set of drums.

"You're here," Ivy cheers when the crowd parts. She crashes into me, pulling me into a hug.

Ivy's been my best friend since our days back in middle school. She always has my back, and I'll always have hers. When I found out Brix, her boyfriend and the lead singer, had made a bet with Tysin, I made it my mission to torture him.

He came to his senses and fought through hell to win her back, but she didn't make it easy on him, that's for sure.

Ivy was offered a job at *Mayhem Magazine* right after college. It's perfect for her since they're allowing her to travel with Brix on the road during the band's tour.

She will have the chance to do what she loves while also supporting his dream.

Their tour, Wreak Some Havoc, is big for them. Not only because they're headlining for the first time but also because most of their shows have sold out.

"I wish you were coming out on the road with me," she mutters against my ear. "What am I gonna do stuck on a bus full of smelly guys for three months?"

She pulls back, wearing a beaming smile on her face.

"You'll have to meet up with us at some of their shows, though. It'll be fun."

Madden sneaks in. "Congratulations, sis." He grunts, pulling me into a side hug. I practically disappear under his muscular arm.

The contrast between the two of us is almost laughable. He stands over a foot taller than me with arms the size of my head.

He slings his arm around my shoulders, pretending to put me in a chokehold. I playfully elbow him in the side before he finally releases me.

"All right, all right." He pushes me back. "Be careful before you take me out and I'm not able to have kids of my own one day."

"Lord help us all," I joke, shaking my head.

"Yo, Madden!" Brix hollers from a few feet away, nodding toward the stage.

"I'm gonna get stuff set up real quick, then I'll be back." He claps me on the shoulder. "I'm proud of you. At least one of us went to college. Pops can be happy with that, right?"

He chuckles, flashing me a wink as he backs away from us and turns to head toward the stage with the guys.

I notice the new guy Madden told me about is tuning his guitar, nodding his head along to the music. Tysin, thankfully, is nowhere in sight.

Canon comes up behind me, wrapping his arm around my waist.

"I'm goin' to grab us some drinks. I'll be right back."

I nod, running my hand over his forearm, and tilt my head up to give him a quick kiss before he disappears.

"I've missed having you at the shows with me," Ivy shouts. It's hard to hear over the music and the sounds of laughter and conversation booming around us.

If I'm being honest, I miss coming to them too. I love watching the guys play, even if it's different now.

"I do too," I say. She wraps her arm around my shoulders, and we sway back and forth to Three Doors Down.

It's been a while since we've hung out, so we use the few minutes we have with just the two of us to catch up. She tells me about how her new job is going and about the tour. They are only a few days away from leaving.

I'm still waiting for the day when Brix proposes. It's only a matter of time before it happens, but they're enjoying their time just the two of them while they can.

"What about you?" She rests her head on her palm. "What's next for you?"

There's a smug look on her face, almost as if she's keeping a secret, and she's bursting at the seams to tell me.

She reaches her hand across the table between us, stopping me midsentence, and tilts her head, signaling to something behind me. When I glance over my shoulder, my eyes land on Canon.

I spin on my heels to face him when he drops to his knee in front of me. All the oxygen is sucked out of my lungs in one quick move.

The music stops, and the crowd turns to face us, the noise level dropping with them. I slap my hand over my mouth, my eyes widening as I stare down at him.

Everything moves in slow motion from there. He holds out the black box in his hand, wearing a beaming smile on his face. He turns his hat backward. Something about that melts me every time he does. The sight of him, kneeling in front of me with the happiness radiating off him, grabs ahold of me.

How could I not want to spend every day for the rest of my life with him?

The energy in the room shifts, urging me to look up. It's almost as if I could feel the heat of Tysin's gaze, but I immediately regret it the moment I do.

My eyes lock on his. His face, his expression, is unreadable. Stoic. Emotionless.

I shake myself out of those thoughts, turning my attention back to Canon. I take a step toward him and bend forward, unable to hear him over the loud cheers and yelps of excitement erupting around us.

"I love you," I whisper against his mouth.

When I pull back, he smiles and presses another quick kiss against my lips.

"Then marry me?"

When Ivy asked me what was next, this is what I want. Canon. He's my future and the person I want to spend my life with.

I may not have a job waiting for me or all the next steps figured out, but I know I want all of it with him.

"Yes." I grin, nodding enthusiastically.

When he stands and wraps his arms around me, his lips crash against mine in a hard kiss. When I close my eyes, letting myself soak in the moment, I see Tysin's face.

Nothing betrays you more than your own mind.

CHAPTER TWO

TYSIN

"Get your shit together, man!" I snarl.

We've been practicing for almost two hours, preparing for our tour. I'm already sick of this new kid.

A Rebels Havoc has had an incredible run for the past two years. We went out on the road last summer with High Octane, and it was the big break we needed. We had labels pounding down our door, wanting a chance to talk to us.

One approached us with an offer we simply couldn't refuse.

Except it came with terms, terms I wasn't too pleased with, like adding a second guitarist to our lineup.

I was ready to wave my middle finger in the air and tell them to stick their contract up their ass.

I didn't, though.

As much as it felt like a dick smack to the face, this is everything I've been dreaming of since I was thirteen years old. It was my final *fuck you* to my mom and everyone in Carolina Beach who ever doubted me.

My love for music and my determination to see us go big won out. If all I have to do is deal with him, I'll grit my teeth and sign on the dotted line.

I still hate how it feels like all my hard work, my dream, was being handed over to him on a silver platter. He doesn't have the respect to appreciate what he's been given.

"Chill out, man!" Brix grunts under his breath.

He notices me take a step toward Trey. Pushing between us, he shoves me on the chest, attempting to calm me down.

"Chill? How would you feel if after you spent hours on lyrics, perfecting your vocals, some kid came in and re-wrote them all?"

Brix understood. We were one and the same. Cut from the same damn cloth.

Madden, on the other hand, is the voice of reason. The calm to our chaos. Whereas I had no filter and zero tolerance for bullshit.

The tension and frustration thrum through me. Brix mutters under his breath to calm down. We're crowded into the small space of our practice studio. It's our second home, the place we've used all those years.

Only now, it's starting to feel like we're crammed into a pressure cooker.

One word and we're all about to explode.

"He's right," Brix says, agreeing with me. He turns, pushing his hand against my chest. His eyes bounce over to Trey, then back to me. "We've busted our ass for the past six months, so we don't need you comin' in here and changing shit right before we leave on tour."

Trey scoffs, rolling his eyes.

"Whatever you say." He holds his hands up, shaking his head. "I didn't realize when I joined that I was gonna be stripped of my balls too. If you want to keep playing out of rhythm, more power to ya."

"Maybe we should call it a day," Madden suggests from behind his drums. His shirt is drenched, and beads of sweat drip down his face.

"Good idea. Tysin needs to go home and take some fuckin' Midol," Brix quips, crossing the room to swipe his bottle of water.

Trey joins in, a smirk stretching across his face.

"Fuck you and you," I jest, pointing at both of them.

We were all in bad moods before we even rolled in here. The truth is, we don't have time to mess around. Our tour starts in less than a week. We came back home to enjoy some downtime before we hit the road.

I was fine with wrapping up for the day. Everything about the past twenty-four hours has me ready to hit Whiskey Barrel for a beer and find someone to take back to my place.

"I need to get home and shower. We have that thing over at your parents' at six," Brix says, taking a large gulp

My eyes bounce over to Madden's, confusion furrowing my brow.

"What thing?" This is the first I've heard of anything going on.

"His parents are throwing a surprise engagement party for Kyla and Canon."

Brix's gaze lingers on me for a moment, trying to gauge my reaction.

As if witnessing it wasn't enough, I saw pictures plastered all over social media this morning.

Yeah, we had a fling. It wasn't anything serious, but it hadn't ended well. Not to mention, she was livid when she found out about the bet between me and Brix and how it hurt Ivy in the process.

She made it clear how much she hates me. Which is fine with me. I don't have any plans to try to change her mind.

In fact, the more she hates me, the easier it is for us to stay the hell away from each other.

Everything about being in CB has me wishing I could leave on tour now. It's only a matter of time before my mom catches wind we're in town. She'll come sniffing around, looking for a handout like she always does. As soon as she heard about our record deal, she was blowing up my phone to the point I blocked her number.

If she thinks for a second I'm giving her a dime, she's outta her damn mind.

Living in LA allowed me to distance myself from this part of my life. I'm ready to hit the road and do the same. With everyone chirping about Kyla's engagement, it couldn't come soon enough.

"You can come by if you want," Madden adds.

He has no idea about my history with his sister. We all knew if he did, it wasn't gonna go over well. He made it clear growing up that dating his sister was off-limits.

Probably because he knew Brix and I weren't the relationship type.

Guess he was wrong about Brix.

It wasn't worth the fight anyway. I got what I wanted out of our time together. The past is better left in the past.

"Nah, man. I think I'm gonna head home, have a few beers, and call it a night."

Madden stands, reaching into his pocket, and pulls out his phone. His brow furrows, a frown appearing on his face at whoever's calling. Brix and Trey are too busy talking about one of the songs we practiced today to notice.

He waves his hand at them, motioning with his finger over his mouth to be quiet before he answers the call.

"Hey, Harper, we're doing good. We just wrapped up a practice session now."

"Yeah, they're all still here. What's going on?"

What the hell is the owner of the record label calling Madden for? Especially so close to the start of our tour.

I pick up on the panic laced in his words, putting me on edge. My eyes bounce from Madden over to Brix. He steps away from Trey, folding his arms and tilting his head forward to listen in.

Madden nods, running his hand over his jaw, his gaze burning holes into my hardwood floors.

"What does this mean on such short notice?" he asks.

Brix flicks his eyes over to me, and I grit my teeth.

"Well, I think I know someone who could help us out. I'd have to talk to her. It's my sister. She graduated from college earlier this month with a degree in business management. While she doesn't have experience in managing a tour, she's been around the band since we started. She knows the ins and outs of what goes on behind the scenes. Plus, I trust her."

What the fuck is he talking about?

"Yeah, I'll see her here in an hour or so. I'll talk to her about it then. What is our backup plan if this doesn't pan out?"

His eyes widen, and he nods his head. I don't want to know her response but judging by the concern on his face, it's not good.

"We'll figure it out. We'll make it happen."

His words were confident and reassuring, but I know Madden. The dread on his face and the tension coiling in his body is anything but relaxed.

He ends the call, and his shoulders slouch in a heavy sigh.

"What was that all about?" Brix asks.

"The tour manager they hired fell through. Family emergency. We're less than a week away, making it hard to find a replacement."

"What's that fuckin' mean?" Brix barks, voicing what we're all thinking.

"She couldn't say, just wanted to let us know. I told her I'd talk to Kyla. She's the only person I could think of who could help us on short notice."

Madden scrubs his hand over his face, and my body goes rigid at the thought.

Three months stuck on a tour bus with Kyla?

Someone hand me a fuckin' beer now because I'm gonna need it.

BOOKS BY BROOKE

A Rebels Havoc Series

Brix
Sins of a Rebel
Tysin
Trey
Madden

Men of Blaze

Personal Foul
Reckless Rebound (Cocky Hero Club)

Tattered Heart Duet

Torn
Tattered

A Heart's Compass Series

Where I Found You
Lost Before You
Until I Found You
Now That I Found You
Where You Belong

Standalones (In order of publication)

Wild Irish

Learn more and purchase your copy at:
www.authorbrookeobrien.com/booksbybrooke

ACKNOWLEDGMENTS

My Boys – I love you more than anything on this earth. Everything I do is for you.

To my AMAZING beta readers – Kristen, Donna, Summer, April, and Ana. Thank you for reading Tysin and Kyla's story before anyone else, for your honest feedback, and helping me make their story better. I'm so grateful for you! <3

Jenny Sims and Rox LeBlanc – I've enjoyed working with and learning from you! Thank you for all your hard work on this project and helping me learn along the way.

To the fantastic bloggers and my Rebel Release Team, thank you for being a part of this one. I'm excited to hear what you think of Tysin and Kyla. I hope you know how grateful I am for every one of you.

My Rebels Readers – I love being able to connect with all of you in my Reader Group and across social media. Thank you for your love of this series. It's truly changed my life and I'm so thankful for you all!

April – Thank you so much for your friendship. We've grown close over the past couple years and I'm so thankful to have you in my life, both as a book friend and a real friend.

Kristen – You keep it real with me, always! I can't begin to put into words how much I appreciate you being there for me. You helped me get this story to where it is today and keeping me focused and motivated in times where I'd never finish. Thanks for riding my ass when I need it, but also reminding me to be patient with myself too.

Kate Jessop and Lyssa Cole – Thank you for your friendship and support, for checking in with me and letting me bounce ideas off you. Your friendship and support mean the world to me.

ABOUT BROOKE

USA Today Bestselling author Brooke O'Brien writes steamy and swoon-worthy new adult romances. She's best known for her sports and rock star romances.

Brooke believes a love worth having is worth fighting for, and she brings this into her stories where her characters risk it all for love.

When she isn't writing or falling in love with a new book boyfriend, you can find her spending time with her family, cheering on her favorite sports teams, listening to ASMR, or binge-watching the latest true crime documentary. She loves rockin' a comfy hoodie with leggings and believes the best days include a good nap.

Brooke loves connecting with readers and hopes you'll join her on her social pages or reader group to stay in touch. To follow Brooke and join her newsletter, visit authorbrookeobrien.com/follow.

COPYRIGHT

Edited by Jenny Sims, Editing4Indies
Proofread by Rox LeBlanc with Rox's Reads
Cover Design by Black Widow Designs
Version: BMO08042023